SENSUOUS

K.M. SCOTT

SENSUOUS

From *New York Times* bestselling author K.M. Scott comes an enemies to lovers romance that shows how thin the line between love and hate truly is.

Alex March is all about having a good time. He loves being single. Life is meant to be enjoyed, and he intends on squeezing as much fun out of this world as he can.

He's living the dream as the head chef at CK, the best restaurant in Tampa, so when he's offered the chance to be on the new cooking reality show Chef on Chef, he figures why not take the chance.

It could be fun.

Kat Truesdale hates Alex from the moment she sees him walk on the set. He's everything she loathes in men. Arrogant, overconfident, and far too good looking, he's one of the golden boys of this world.

The reality show is a competition for a million-dollar prize, and she intends on walking away the winner. Alex may think he's got this in the bag, but not if Kat has anything to say about it.

Let the games begin!

Sensuous is a work of fiction. Names, characters, places, and events are the products of the author's imagination. Any resemblance to events, locations, or persons, living or dead, is coincidental.

2022 Copper Key Media LLC

Published in the United States

ISBN: 978-1-955335-15-7

CHAPTER ONE

lex

THE USUAL RACKET IN THE KITCHEN AT CK ON A busy Saturday night nearly drowns out my thoughts about what I should do after work tonight. Cade practically begged me to drop in at the club, but that's only because now that he's a committed man, there's nothing there for him other than actual work, and he's never been a big fan of that.

Unlike me. Not that I don't enjoy a good night out, but there's nothing I love more than being here in my kitchen doing what I do best.

Lost in thought about Cade and his desperate pleas to get me to go to Club X tonight, I don't hear Kane talking to me until he taps me on the shoulder.

K.M. SCOTT

Confused for a second, I turn to look at him and shake my head.

"What's up?"

"I called your name twice. You looked like you were a million miles away there, Alex," he says with a smile.

Shrugging, I shake my head. "Nothing terribly deep. Just what I plan to do after work. Did you need something?"

Kane points toward the kitchen doors that lead out to the dining room. "You've got someone to see you. They're sitting at eighty-six."

I set down my knife and slip off my gloves, more than a little curious. "Someone to see me, huh? Any clue who it is?"

My uncle wouldn't necessarily know since he's not expected to keep a running catalog of the women I see, but he tends to slyly notice things like that. He shakes his head, though, which could mean a perfect stranger is out there waiting for me or just someone who knows me who hasn't come around the restaurant before this.

"Well, do you know what they want?" I ask with more than a hint of impatience as he stands in my way of getting to the sink.

With a shake of his head, he says, "Nope. They just asked for you. I assume they loved the salmon?"

Sometimes I can't tell when Kane's joking and when he's dead serious. Like at this moment as his blue eyes stare into mine, I honestly don't know if he's taking a shot at my cooking or genuinely thinks a customer wants to speak to me about the salmon.

Either way, I guess I'm going to find out when I meet them.

As I step around him, I slip off my hat and run my hands through my hair. "I guess I better get out there then. My adoring public awaits."

That makes him laugh, giving me the hint it's probably a woman waiting for me. Still, I have no idea who it could be. I don't recall inviting anyone to the restaurant for tonight.

I wash my hands and then make my way across the kitchen and head out into the dining room, my attention focused on the best table in the house. Eighty-six. The maître d' only sits important people at that table, unless someone asks for it specifically. Nestled next to the far wall of windows that look out on the water, it's the most secluded and intimate spot in the restaurant.

I'm surprised to see not a woman or even a couple but two men and a woman seated there. For a second, I imagine maybe they've got some ménage thing going on after dinner. It's not out of the realm of possibility.

But as I approach the table, I dismiss that idea as improbable based on the way the three of them are dressed. Both men wear dark business suits, while the woman is dressed in a black skirt and silver silk blouse with a bow. Attractive, they don't look like they've ever gotten freaky a day in their lives, which makes my ménage idea unlikely. Possibly, since you can never truly tell a book by its cover, but unlikely.

The three people appear to be in their mid-to-late forties, I'm guessing. The woman has nearly jet-black hair that just barely hits her shoulders and big brown eyes, the kind that seem to swallow you up. The two men have what I call business faces—they look like they spend too much time making money instead of doing anything. The hint of gray I see at both their temples makes me wonder if they might be a few years older than my initial guess.

What they could want with me I have no idea. Maybe Kane was right. Perhaps they did like the salmon.

I stop next to the man seated closest to the window and put on my nicest company-man smile. "Hello, I'm Alex March, the head chef here at CK. I'm told you wanted to speak to me?"

For a long second, all three of them stare up at me like they're examining every inch of my face. Did Kane get the table number wrong? He's usually good about remembering things like that, though.

I notice the woman's gaze trail down my body and wonder what the hell is going on, but then the man sitting next to me smiles and nods, followed by his two friends. Whatever they want, it has nothing to do with the salmon since a quick glance at their plates tells me none of them had that entrée for dinner.

"Alex March, it's great to meet you!" the man

4

says with far more enthusiasm than I expected. Extending his hand to shake mine, he continues, "Please let me introduce myself and my colleagues. I'm Shane Kimball, and this is Jonathan Ridge and Maria Sanchez. Do you have a few moments to talk?"

Maria continues to scan my body like some horny schoolgirl, which makes sitting down with these people nothing I really want to do, but out of the corner of my eye, I see my father and Kane looking at me from across the room and know I have to be nice.

Forcing a smile, I nod. "Sure. I have a few minutes. Was there something wrong with your entrées?"

The three of them shake their heads, and the woman who's been checking me out so hard I half expect her to cop a feel on me at any moment says, "Oh, no! Everything was incredible. That's part of why we wanted to speak to you."

What the other part could be I instantly wonder since she's returned to giving me the once over, but I take the empty seat at the table and force another smile for them. "I'm happy to hear that. So what can I do for you tonight?"

For the first time, Jonathan speaks up, and I'm instantly impressed with how deep his voice is. Like someone who sounds like Darth Vader deep.

"Alex, we're the producers for an upcoming reality show Chef on Chef for the Food and Leisure

Network. Are you familiar with reality cooking shows?"

I feel my smile begin to fade as he speaks. Yes, I'm familiar with them, and no, I don't watch them. I'm not interested in any show that creates drama for drama's sake while trying to make people feel like shit because they can't make a decent dish out of crap someone found in the back of their grandmother's pantry.

"Not really. I'm sure I've caught a few of them over time, but I don't really go in for that kind of thing."

As I finish speaking, I see my father with his gaze full of curiosity staring at me, so I quickly add, "Then again, I don't have much time to go in for anything since I'm here almost every night."

Shane reaches across the table and slaps me on the forearm. "Well, no matter. It might be better if you have no real experience with shows like ours, to be honest, for what we have in mind."

I still have no idea what the hell any of them are talking about and I need to return to my kitchen, so I nod and smile. Hopefully, they'll start talking plainly any moment now.

"Here's the thing, Alex," Maria says. "We've heard great things about you, and after eating our dinners, we can see you clearly know what you're doing. You're also exactly what we're looking for in a chef to participate in our show. You're talented, good-looking, and I'm betting viewers will adore you."

"Adore me doing what?" I ask, already having a sick feeling in my stomach about what I believe she's going to say next.

With a big, toothy smile, she answers, "Competing for a million-dollar prize."

Her words hit my ears strangely, so I repeat what she said. "A million-dollar prize?"

"Yes. Chef on Chef will have eight contestants competing for a million dollars to start their own restaurant. We know you're happy here since it's your family's business, but think about what a million dollars could do for you, Alex. You could go out on your own and establish your very own restaurant."

I turn to look over at my father and wonder if he'd be so happy if he knew what these people were proposing. Not that I have any plans to strike out on my own. Why would I when I'm going to have this business sometime in the future? It's not like Cash, Liam, or Wilder have any interest in CK, and both my father and Kane have already started talking about when they'll be walking away from the business.

"As much as I'm flattered to be considered, I don't think I'm exactly right for this show of yours. Thanks for the offer, though."

Before I can stand to leave, Shane grabs my arm from across the table to stop me. "Hang on. Hear us out. As Maria said, you're perfect. You're known as a talented chef, and you're exactly what viewers will want to see in a contestant."

"Again, I'm flattered, but no thanks. Good luck with the show, though."

"Take my card then," Jonathan says in that deep supervillain voice of his. "If you reconsider, call me. Don't miss out on a chance of a lifetime."

Just to be polite, I take his business card and smile as both Shane and Maria hand me theirs. I thank them again since I don't want my disinterest in their reality show to hurt the restaurant and head back toward my kitchen. By the time I reach my father, he's nearly bursting to know what it was all about and follows me back through the doors.

"So that looked interesting. I saw they gave you their cards. What's up?"

Tossing all three business cards onto my table where I keep my stuff while I'm working, I laugh at how curious he is. "Well, if you must know, they want to steal me away and give me my own restaurant," I joke.

"What? Really?" he says in a voice of pure shock.

"Sort of. They want me to be on some reality show. I thought the woman was going to lick me at one point, which was more than a little creepy, to be honest. I turned them down, of course. I don't have any interest in reality shows."

"What would this show be about?" my father asks as he studies me all wide-eyed like I'm different now that three strangers think I'd be perfect for their reality cooking show.

Standing at my station again, I slip on my hat and gloves again to get back to work. As I pick up my knife, I shrug. "I don't know. It's called Chef on Chef. Sounds more like porn than anything to do with food."

"Hmmm…you know, your mother watches those things. I've walked through the living room while they've been on sometimes. They always mention the restaurants the people work at. It could be good for business here, Alex."

I glance up and down the line full of busy chefs making food for a packed house and then turn to look at him. "As if we're struggling here in any way? I'm betting if I went out to check the reservations that we're booked solid for months. Speaking of that, how did those three get in tonight? Did you have something to do with that?"

My father raises his hands as if to surrender. "Not me. Maybe Kane, but I swear I didn't know a thing about it."

"Well, I'm not interested in any of it, so Mom is going to have to watch a crop of strangers cook when it finally airs."

As I get back to making food, he leans in and says in my ear, "Not even if there might be beautiful female contestants?"

Slowly, I turn my head to stare him down. "You know, just because Cash, Liam, and Cade are all settled down now doesn't mean I want to be. I can find beautiful woman anywhere, Dad. I don't need to go on some reality show to do it."

Again, he puts his hands up, but this time he smiles. "Nobody's trying to get you to settle down. If anything, I just wanted to point out that you might find some potential girlfriends who share the same interests as you do."

"Don't worry about me finding potential girlfriends. There's no shortage of them in my life, so I'm good."

Likely sensing he can't change my mind about this reality show nonsense, he walks away, leaving me to my job I already love. I don't need to be on some drama-filled reality show pretending to hate other contestants while I attempt to make some dish from lima beans, quinoa, and a sauce some jackass producer thinks would be funny to include.

No thanks. I'm good right here in the kitchen of CK where I've been since I graduated from culinary school and where I'll be until I own this place sometime in the future.

at

I LEAN BACK AGAINST MY NOT-SO-WONDERFUL couch with the weird spring that pinches your hip that my mother and father so kindly gave me five years ago when I started working right out of culinary school. Staring at the business card that Jonathan guy gave me, I have to admit a million dollars could solve nearly all my problems.

And any left over would be a lot easier to deal with if I had that much money.

"So are you going to do it or not? I personally think you should," my roommate Sadie says, interrupting my fantasies about what I'd do with a million dollars.

Setting the card on the coffee table in front of me, I try to play it cool so she doesn't go over the top with this whole thing. "I'm seriously considering it. It could be fun, and I know my boss would be willing to give me time off in exchange for some free promo on the show."

Sadie jumps up out of her chair and excitedly waves her arms in the air. "You're going to be famous! This is so great!"

So much for trying to keep my friend from going overboard.

"It's just a local thing, Sadie. These are the prelims. I'd have to win this local competition and then win the regional and national ones to be famous."

Her shoulders sag so she looks somewhat deflated as she sits down on the chair again. "Then you'll be locally famous. That's still pretty great. Have you thought about what you want to do when you win the million dollars? Just remember us little people when you get big, okay?"

Looking around our mediocre apartment, I smile. "I promise if I win that we're moving to a nicer place. Maybe somewhere down near the bay."

Sadie's blue eyes get big at the mention of new digs. "Oooooh, a great place where we could have parties and invite hot men to hang out with us?"

Waving that idea away, I chuckle. "I'll leave the hot men and party planning to you. I'd just like somewhere with a great view. Wouldn't that be nice?"

"Somewhere I can lay out and get some sun without guys like those creepy brothers down the hall constantly coming out to gawk would be so great, Kat. Do you know the last time I tried to get some sun they sat out on the grass and made a running commentary about how I looked in my bikini? What assholes!"

The Prescott brothers are pure pervs, no doubt. I'm pretty sure they live with their parents, even though they've got to be in their thirties, and they never fail to make some lewd comment every time they see Sadie or me. They think that will endear them to us.

They're wrong.

"I swear if I win we're moving to a better place."

That brings a smile back to Sadie's face. "When. Not if you win but when. You're a fantastic chef, Kat. Wait until those producer people get a load of what you can do."

As much as I want to think I could win this cooking show competition, I'm secretly worried the other contestants will be from much better restaurants. Frederick's isn't bad, but it's no five-star place. I'm not even sure we'd rate four stars on some days, to be honest.

"Well, I guess I'll find out soon."

"Tell me again what they said. How many contestants will there be? Did they tell you any names? We could go scope out the competition since tonight's your night off. I am a little hungry. Actually,

I'm a little thirsty. Let's go out and get a drink to celebrate your good fortune!"

Before I can say no to that suggestion since the last thing I want to do is go club hopping on my night off, Sadie is off like a shot toward her bedroom. "I'm going to wear that purple dress I bought a while back. Now that I have something that resembles a tan and I don't look like some sick Victorian woman who's hoping to escape typhus, it's going to look incredible!" she yells out.

"I'm really not sure I want to go out tonight. It's my only night off all week, and I'm feeling pretty beat."

Damn, that sounds pathetic. Twenty-five-year-old women shouldn't sound so sad. It's just that I only have one night away from work, and I'd planned on relaxing tonight.

Sadie pokes her head out from behind her bedroom door and scowls. "Seriously, what is wrong with you, girl? We never go out anymore. That needs to stop tonight. Between our two jobs, we've forgotten what having a good time feels like. So get dressed in something hot and let's go! Should I go for sexy beach waves or leave my hair straight?"

Reluctantly, I stand up and head toward my bedroom to do as she's ordered. "Leave it straight. Your hair looks great that way. The light bounces off your highlights and makes your brown hair look even better when you go straight."

"Awww, that's so nice of you to say. I was worried I was having a shitty hair day, but now you've made me feel all warm and cuddly inside."

"Glad I could help. Any suggestions on what I should wear?" I ask, half-heartedly joking. Sadie's taste is definitely not like mine. I think the only dresses I own are all black.

I'm hooked up for funerals until the end of the decade or until I either lose a lot of weight or gain a bunch.

Knowing me all too well, she laughs and says, "Well, maybe something black? Seriously, though, go with the strapless dress you wore to Devon's wedding. That's a good look on you. All that chopping vegetables does wonders for your arms, so show those babies off!"

She isn't wrong. At least there's that benefit from being a chef at Frederick's. I just wish I could move up the ladder at the restaurant, but with Deidre as head chef, that's never going to happen at my current job.

After slipping into the dress Sadie suggested, I take a good hard look in the mirror. Nice arms, if I do say so myself. Not a bad face either. I should wear those false eyelashes my mother sent me last week. They would make my eyes pop.

Why bother, though? I'm doing this for Sadie, not to meet some mythical hot guy who's perfect for me. I've already decided that man doesn't exist, so there's no point in wishing for the impossible.

. . .

NOT FIVE STEPS INTO CLUB X AND I ALREADY WISH I was back at the apartment watching some serial killer documentary. The music is so loud I can't hear myself think, and I've already been touched by too many strangers for this to be a good time.

Sadie thrives in places like this. Wide-eyed, she scans the room for hot guys, one of her favorite pastimes. Unlike me, she hasn't given up on love. In fact, it's the single thing on her mind most days, even though she's had her fair share of lame guys waltz through her life.

How she keeps believing is beyond me.

Grabbing my hand, she gives it a squeeze and starts pulling me toward the bar. "Don't just stand there like a pole. Let's get a drink and check things out. I've seen about a dozen guys I'm liking already, including that man in the suit standing over near the wall. What do you think?"

I look around to see this man she's talking about, and there near what looks like the office door across from the bar area down here on the main floor stands a very attractive man who I'm guessing has to be twice Sadie's age. Is that the one she's talking about?

"Have you decided to have daddy issues now?" I ask as she continues to drag me through the crowd. "He could be your father, honey."

She turns to look back at him and smiles. "I don't

think so. He just has a vibe about him that makes it seem like he's older. I'm guessing he's not even forty, which is absolutely in my age range for potential boyfriends."

By the time we get to the bar, she's given me half a dozen reasons why older men are better lovers and how she thinks they could have a good time tonight. She is wearing that purple dress, which she claims is her get lucky dress, so maybe it could happen.

Whatever floats her boat. I'm not interested in any men, old or young, so who am I to say anything about her choices?

The attractive man behind the bar who sort of resembles the older guy over near the wall takes our drink order from her, and I nudge her in the side. Leaning in, I say in her ear, "This guy looks like your dream man across the room. Coincidence?"

Sadie narrows her eyes in disgust and stares at me. "Don't ruin this. I have an entire fantasy going with that guy, and now you want to say he could be this guy's father? No way."

When the bartender serves our drinks, I lean across the bar and say above the way too loud music, "The guy over near the wall—a relative or does this place just hire men who look like you two?"

He gives me a very sexy smile and nods. "That's Stefan March, the owner of Club X and my father. Cade March, at your service."

I throw my head back and laugh at the sight of

Sadie's crestfallen expression from the news that her dream man is, in fact, old enough to be her father. "Told you!"

Trying to salvage anything good from this turn of events, she asks the bartender, "Any chance Daddy isn't married to Mommy or step-Mommy?"

With another great smile, he shakes his head. "Sorry, he and my mother have been married for over twenty-five years. He's crazy about her."

Sadie clings to one last hope as she sighs and asks, "And you, Cade? Happily married too?"

"Not yet, but there's a beautiful baker who stole my heart a while ago. Sorry. I have a cousin who looks just like my father and me, though. I think he's coming by tonight, so stick around."

When he walks away, I give her a hug to cheer her up. "There's still hope. Maybe the cousin's genes will work for you. These two do have a good look about them, so don't give up yet."

With a pout, she nods. "I'm worried you're right and there are no good ones out there. So much for having a good night. Now all I can do is get drunk."

"That's the spirit. We'll get drunk, dance, and have a good time. Who needs men to do any of that?"

That brings a smile to her face, and she lifts her glass in the air to make a toast. "Exactly! Who needs men? They're only good for one thing, right?"

I tap the rim of my glass off hers and nod my

agreement. "Right, and we have BOBs for that, so fuck 'em!"

"Here's to BOB!" Sadie yells over the music. "He better be charged up because I'm going to be ready to go tonight!"

Yet another disappointed woman who believes in her vibrator over the males of the world is welcomed to the club. It's okay. BOB never disappoints, assuming he's got fresh batteries. Sadie's just going to have to work out her daddy issues that way.

CHAPTER THREE

lex

By the time I get to the club, it's after one and I'm just about the only sober person in the building, excluding the Club X staff and my uncle who never seems to drink lately. I see Cade upstairs at the second-floor bar and make my way up through the crowd of people who've chosen to use the stairs as their personal resting place.

Actually, most of them seem to be halfway to fucking, so it's not truly resting what they're doing. I step over one couple practically blocking the entire step right before I reach the second floor and laugh when the beautiful woman looks up at me with pure lust in her glassy eyes.

Not tonight, honey. I'm here to get a buzz on and forget how hard I fucking worked tonight, not steal some guy's drunk date from him.

"There he is! The man of the hour," Cade calls out to me as I look back at the couple from the stairs and see the woman smiling at me.

"It seems I am. What are you putting in the drinks tonight? She looks like she's about to bail on the guy working so hard to get in her pants for me."

He laughs and pushes a glass of whiskey neat toward me across the bar. "I've got one even better than that. Some girl I'm guessing in her mid-twenties, sober too, was asking questions about none other than Stefan March himself earlier tonight. Seems she's into his look since when she heard he was happily married she wanted to know if I was available. I had to disappoint her, but I put in a good word for you."

Just then, the owner of Club X appears next to me at the bar and slaps me on the back. "How are you, Alex? We don't see you around here enough these days. What's been keeping you away?"

I take a quick gulp of my drink and shrug. "Your son is busy being committed to Hailey, so I'm on my own now."

"Don't blame me because you choose to not have a social life these past few months. I'm here like I've been for over a year. You're just a workaholic lately," Cade says as he fulfills the drink order for a nice-looking brunette in a short skirt that shows off her great legs.

My gaze lingers on her for a few moments before she walks away, and I start to tell Cade and Stefan about what happened with those reality show producers tonight. "Get a load of this. Three people come into the restaurant for a late dinner, and they ask to see me."

Before I can go any further, Cade jokes, "Busy burning dinner again, dear? You know that upsets customers."

"Fuck off and listen, okay?"

That makes both of my relatives stop laughing, and Stefan slaps me on the back again. "Cade's in rare form tonight. Better watch it."

"I'm not the one with women half my age checking me out, so who's in rare form tonight?" Cade says with a chuckle, and for a second, I have a sense that my uncle might be a little embarrassed by his comment.

"Half your age would barely be a teenager, so I should hope not," Stefan says with a chuckle.

This father-son thing they have going makes telling my story next to impossible until they get this out of their system, so I settle in with my drink and look down at the action happening on the first floor while they bust each other's balls for the next few minutes. There are a few interesting prospects, but by this time of the night, they're likely way too drunk to be anything but a sloppy lay. I'm not in the mood for that tonight.

Stefan leans in next to me and wraps his arm around my shoulders. "Sorry, Alex. I guess we're both in rare form tonight."

I shake my head and smile. In all honesty, it's good to see Cade and his father getting along like this. For far too long, they were more like enemies than family, so I don't mind listening to their ball-busting.

"It's okay. It gave me time to check out the women here tonight. So are you two ready to hear my story? I promise it's a good one."

"As long as it has nothing to do with Kane," Stefan says, rolling his eyes.

Unsure what he means, I look across the bar at Cade for some explanation. "What's that about?"

"They're in a fight to the death about something that happened at Grandma's last time we were all out there. Remember Kane saying something about the whole Christmas thing and how this year it would be at his and Abbi's house and he'd be playing Santa Claus?"

"For who? Ava's the youngest, and she's already old enough to drink."

Stefan jumps back into the conversation, way more heated than he was just a few minutes ago. "It's not the point. It's the principal of the thing. I'm always Santa Claus, and now he's acting like just because Christmas will be at their house this year that he's suddenly going to be the star of the show. I swear he does this shit to get under my skin. I'm the King of Christmas. Period. Full stop. Kane can be one of my goddamned elves."

As I work to stifle my chuckle, he storms away, throwing his arms up in the air. When he's far enough from the bar, Cade and I burst into laughter. Our family really is fucked up.

"He's been like that for weeks," Cade says, shaking his head. "Maybe they should fight it out. That might put an end to all of this nonsense."

"I doubt it," I say and take another drink of whiskey. "So let me get this story out because I have to tell someone since it's so wild. So these three producers from some cooking channel come into the restaurant tonight and say they want to talk to me. Turns out they want me to be on some reality show. Can you believe that? What the hell would I want to do that for?"

Oddly, Cade doesn't look like he finds any of this as amusing as I do. As he mixes a gin and tonic for some guy I think I saw on the stairs coming up here, he says, "Is there some monetary benefit to doing it? If there is, it could be fun."

"For someone like you. You love that shit. I bet they found me because you roped me into that ridiculous bachelor auction for charity last month. You do know the woman who won the bid for me was like seventy, don't you?"

Throwing his head back in peals of laughter, he

pushes the glass to the drunk guy at the end of the bar before turning his attention back to me. "Did you do her?"

"Fuck you. Did you do the woman who bought you?"

"No, but not because she wasn't hot. I didn't do her because I'm madly in love with Hailey. You have no such excuse."

"I don't need an excuse. I don't recall being told participating in the auction meant I had to fuck the winner."

"Well, there's always the woman from earlier tonight who seems to like the dark hair and brown eyes look we have going on with our side of the family."

Cade looks down at the people on the first floor and points at two women standing near the bar. "There! She's the one in purple. Not bad. I could see you with her."

I follow where his finger is pointing and see two women, one in purple and one in black. Both are beautiful.

"Best friends, I'm betting," I say with a smile.

"One's nice, but two can be even better," Cade says with a knowing chuckle.

"And you say she was into your father first? Not sure I want sloppy seconds," I joke.

"Sloppy thirds," he corrects me as his replacement slides behind the bar. "She was into me for about a nanosecond until she found out I was taken."

"And the friend?" I ask as he starts heading for the stairs.

With a shit-eating grin, he answers, "She was teasing her about having daddy issues. I don't think she was into our look at all, strangely enough."

I follow him to the stairs and give the woman at the top of the steps a wink and a smile as we pass. "Go figure. She must not have any taste at all."

Throwing his hands up, he laughs. "I know, right? Probably likes fucking blond guys with blue eyes who look like surfers or some shit like that."

When we reach the first floor, he nudges me toward the two women. "I'd introduce you, but I didn't get their names. Jesus, I really am a hopeless cause."

"That's what love does to you. I'm okay without an introduction. I'll just drop your father's name and I'll be in with the one who likes old guys."

Cade's eyebrows shoot up into his forehead at my not-so-subtle jab. "Well, now I hope you don't get either of them for that crack, fucker."

"At least you know you'll still have it when you're Stefan's age, right?"

Shaking his head, he turns to walk toward the office, leaving me to my own devices. While I walk over to them, I can't help but notice they're both pretty hot. Maybe if the one who's into our side of the family's look doesn't work out then the other one might.

Just before I reach them, the woman in the purple dress sees me and her eyes grow wide. She really does have a thing for dark hair and brown eyes, I guess.

"Are you the cousin of the bartender from before?" she asks as I join the two of them.

"Yeah. Cade's my cousin and the owner of this place is my uncle. I'm Alex, Alex March," I say with a smile as I size up the two women in front of me.

"I'm Sadie," the woman in purple says before turning to her friend. "And this is Katerina."

The one in the black dress corrects her. "Kat, actually."

"Nice to meet you two. I've never seen you here at Club X before. First time?"

"Yes, and I love it! It's so full of fun people. My friend doesn't like it so much, though. Too noisy for her."

I turn to look at Kat and see her attempt a smile. It ends up more like a grimace than anything happy, though.

"Sadie's more of the club kind. I'm more of the hang out at home kind. Boring, I know, but after a long day at work, the last thing I want to do is deal with people."

"I work as an assistant to the CEO of Starling, and Kat is a chef at Frederick's across town. What do you do?"

My ears perk up at hearing one of them actually does something in the business I'm in, but the look on Kat's face quickly turns from a slight grimace to a downright glare for her friend at the mention of her job. I don't know much about the restaurant she works at, but she clearly didn't want Sadie to tell me what she does for a living.

"I'm the head chef at CK," I answer and then turn to look at Kat who's practically cringing now. "You don't like working as a chef? We've got some great people in that position at my restaurant."

"It's fine. Excuse me, please."

Sadie and I watch her walk away, and my curiosity about why she left gets the better of me. I turn back to look at her friend and ask, "Was it something I said?"

Frowning, she answers, "She's not happy at her job. She's a really great chef, but her boss keeps giving promotions to other people who got hired after her. It's not fair. Just because Kat isn't a kiss ass she punishes her every time there's an opening."

"That must suck," I mumble, silently thanking my luck at having family who own a restaurant I can work in.

"I better go find her. I'm sorry, Alex. It was nice to meet you, though."

"It was nice to meet you too."

And with that, Sadie runs off in the direction of the bathrooms to find her unhappy friend. Cade appears at my side a few seconds later with another drink for me and his trademark sensitivity.

"Struck out with both of them? Jesus, Alex. The one in purple wanted to do my father. You must be losing your touch."

Lifting my glass to my lips, I consider telling him to fuck off, but maybe he's right. Maybe I have lost my touch. Or maybe neither one of them was what I wanted tonight.

I shrug and let him have his fun. "I'm not crying over it. Women are a dime a dozen, Cade. You'd remember that if you didn't have your dick tied in a knot."

Suddenly, all the fun leaves his expression. "Dude, I thought you liked Hailey."

"I do. She's one of my favorite people."

Relief washes over him, and he sits down on a barstool next to where I'm standing. "Oh, good. I thought for a second there that we had a problem. I'm not sure what I'd do if you and she didn't get along."

Christ, he can be so stupid sometimes.

"What you'd do is continue living your life and being happy with the woman of your dreams. What the hell is wrong with you?"

"Well, I guess I would, but the thought of my best friend and my girlfriend hating one another sounds pretty fucking terrible."

I pat him on the shoulder in an attempt to comfort him since this clearly bothers him. "Don't worry,

Cade. Sometimes I like Hailey even more than I like you."

A big grin lights up his face, and my favorite cousin shakes his head. "Fuck you."

After a few moments of listening to the music, I hear him say, "So seriously, you struck out with both of them? Doesn't this worry you?"

"You sound like my father. Why the hell is everyone so damn interested in me finding someone? I'm blaming you, my brother, and Liam. I'm single and happy about it. So what if I didn't get those women tonight? Tomorrow's another day."

"Okay, onto another topic. I think you should do that reality cooking show."

I turn to look at him in confusion. "Why the hell should I do that? I don't even watch reality TV."

Cade waves away that excuse and rolls his eyes. "What does that matter? Are they going to pay you?"

"No, but there's a chance to win a million dollars, so I guess that's sort of like getting paid for the person who wins," I explain, still baffled that Cade thinks I should do this stupid show.

"You could open your own restaurant for that kind of cash, man. I say you do it."

"That assumes I don't have a restaurant that I'm going to get when my father and Kane retire."

Another eye roll comes in response to that statement of fact. "Do you want to wait until they decide to quit working to have your own restaurant?

Imagine it. No Kane hiring only people his age with a million years of experience. Running the entire place your way instead of their way. It would be great, wouldn't it?"

It would be nice to work with someone close to my age. That will happen when I take over CK, though.

"I can see by the look on your face that you're thinking about it," Cade says with a knowing smile. He's had to listen to me complain about how there's no one even close to my age in the kitchen more than once.

"What's the worst that can happen if you do this? You're the best at what you do. Show it off and win some money."

"Something tells me I'm going to regret it if I do this," I say with a laugh.

"Don't be ridiculous. The only time you regret things is when you don't do them. That's the hedonist in you. So go do it and have some fun."

Maybe he's right. What's the worst that can happen? I can handle a little drama, I guess, and it's a reality cooking show. I'll do what I do best and win some good money.

"And regarding your inability to get a woman, you can just keep telling people you're single because you like being a bachelor."

I shake my head at his need to bust my balls. "Fuck you."

Cade throws his head back and laughs. "That wouldn't solve your problem."

After I toss back the rest of my whiskey, I set the glass down on the bar to leave. "Thanks for the drinks. We should do this again sometime. You know, when you're allowed to come out and play."

Cade takes my less than subtle dig with the right attitude and rolls his eyes. "You're just jealous. You wish you had someone like Hailey."

I wave off his comment as I turn to head toward the door. He's not entirely wrong, though. It would be nice to have someone who knows about my job to spend time with. Since I work with chefs who are all Kane's age after he decided a minimum of ten years' experience was absolutely necessary to work at CK, it's not like I'm going to find anyone at work.

Then again, I've never met a woman who makes me want to settle down, and I work constantly, so finding the one like Cade, Liam, and Cash have seems unlikely.

CHAPTER FOUR

at

My hands tremble as the group of us wait for the last contestant to arrive on the set, so I hide them behind my back in the hope that no one will see how nervous I am. I don't know what the stories of the rest of the people are, but mine includes being downright desperate to get enough money to move the hell out of my current position at the restaurant and out of the apartment Sadie and I share with nosy neighbors and creeps who watch us sunbathe.

I nervously glance around at the other people I'll be competing against and have to stifle the urge to burst into tears. I can do this. Sadie's right. I am a good cook. The producers of the show wouldn't have approached me to audition if they didn't think I had a chance to win the million-dollar prize.

All I need to do is believe in myself.

And then *he* walks in, and all my confidence evaporates into thin air.

Alex March. Head chef at CK, one of the premier restaurants in the entire Tampa area. Confident as all hell and for good reason. He's gorgeous, charming, and possibly the most talented chef I've ever heard of.

He has no idea, but I had the chance to experience his cooking one time my parents came to town to visit me. It was the best meal I've ever had, and my father, the man who's been the head chef at some of the finest restaurants in New York City, couldn't rave enough about the food. He even asked the chef to come out to see us to gush over his talent, but I hurried off to the ladies' room because I couldn't stand hearing my own father heap such praise on a perfect stranger while he's never said even a single word about anything I've ever made him.

And to think I had the nerve to say Sadie has daddy issues.

"Ladies and gentlemen, our final contestant has finally joined us, so come in close and we'll get started," the man named Jonathan says in that deep voice of his.

Alex flashes a sexy smile as he walks over toward where the rest of us have gathered. "Sorry about being late. I got tied up with someone at work and couldn't get away."

With one of his many admirers, for sure. Or maybe he had some woman servicing him and he didn't want to leave before he finished.

The nicest of the three producers and the one I like most, Shane, smiles at me and begins giving us his pep talk. "Okay, we've got a great group here, so we're looking forward to a fantastic time on Chef on Chef. You've all gotten contracts you've signed, so you know how this is going to go. You'll get to know one another as time goes on, and in my opinion, that makes things more realistic."

The third producer, Maria, lets out a tiny laugh and says with a smile, "As if that has anything to do with what we do."

"Just a little refresher about how this is scripted. We're going to watch you all this week and then see what kind of plotlines we can come up with. Reality shows have nothing to do with reality, so keep that in mind. We know how to make good TV, so you do what you do best, and let us do our thing. Okay, everyone has a station they've been assigned to, so head there now and let's make some reality TV magic!"

My head down, I walk around looking for my place and find it near the center of the room. That's a good sign, I guess. Then I look over at who they put in the middle of all the action, and I see Alex March standing there looking like he belongs nowhere else in the world.

I shouldn't be jealous. So what if he's so talented my own father who I've emulated my entire life thinks he's the best chef he's ever encountered in his entire thirty-year career as a chef?

As I busy myself getting my area set up to my preferences, I hear him say, "Hey, you're the woman from Club X last week. I'm glad to see a familiar face here. Kat, right?"

Jesus, he sounds so affable and friendly that I can't just ignore him, so I lift my head and force a smile. "Hi. Yeah, Kat. You're Alex March, right?"

As if I don't know that name as well as my own.

With a winning smile that goes perfectly with his stunning good looks, he says, "Good luck!"

All I hear when he says those words is, "I'm going to win this whole thing hands down, but nice to see you came out to try your best." Instantly, I feel my mouth turn down into a frown. I want to snap back that any of us have a chance to win this competition, but I stuff my angry words down deep inside and turn my attention back to my own station.

For the next hour, the eight of us contestants busy ourselves making our favorite dish. When Shane announced that would be our job for the day, I immediately felt a rush of happiness go through me. Nobody makes a better pesto herb chicken entrée than

I do. I've even won awards for my basil pesto. I got this.

At some point, I realize someone's staring at me, and I look up to see Alex smiling. Why the hell is he smiling at me?

"What?" God, this person makes me feel so insecure. I hate that!

"We're both making the same dish. Herb chicken with pesto sauce. Yours looks incredible. Lots of pine nuts. They smell fantastic."

Never in my life have I felt so disheartened. The same exact dish? How could that happen? That's his favorite thing to make? Why? They have every meat and vegetable available to mankind here on this set, and he chooses chicken?

Fuck me. This man is my nemesis. I think I hate him.

No. There's no thinking about it. I know I hate him.

"Yeah, pine nuts. Thanks," I mutter as all the joy in my body disappears.

And here I thought this would turn out well.

When our time is up, Shane and Maria walk around the room tasting each dish and raving about every one of them. When they get to me, I paste a smile on my face and hold my breath as the two people I desperately want to impress take a sample of my pesto herb chicken with cherry tomatoes.

"This is wonderful, Kat," Shane says with enough enthusiasm for me to believe he's telling the truth.

Relief washes over me, and I smile even more broadly. "Thank you. It's one of my favorite meals to make."

"It really is delicious," Maria says as she takes a second forkful. "You do something unique with pine nuts, don't you?"

I nod but don't say what that something unique is. It's a family secret, and I don't plan on sharing that anytime soon.

When they move to Alex's station, I notice he's smiling at me. It's probably just his way of gloating because he knows his version of the dish is infinitely better than mine.

For the next three minutes, I listen to Shane and Maria compliment him on his effort and hear the words that never fail to crush me when my father says them about anyone else's food but mine.

"This is the best thing I've tasted all week," Maria gushes as she touches his arm and basically flirts with him.

Everyone trains their gazes on the wonderful Alex March, but all I can do is focus on the pathetic meal on the plate in front of me. How could I ever think that I'd have any chance to win this competition?

Maria and Shane walk away raving about his pesto sauce, clearly unimpressed with my secret with the pine nuts that makes mine unique. One of their assistants scurries around the room collecting all the dishes the eight of us made, and when the young redheaded girl gets to my station, she gives me a meek smile.

Even she knows I was utterly overshadowed by Alex's effort. Ugh. Unpaid interns feel like they should pity me now. I'm never going to win this competition with him around.

"Okay, we loved what we saw with that," Shane says enthusiastically. "Great! Now we want to get to know each one of you and see how you work with the camera when it's only you. Ready? Because this is going to be much harder than cooking for you guys, so brace yourselves. When your name is called, come over to the side of the set and be ready to divulge your deepest and darkest secrets. And everyone else can feel free to watch."

Maria elbows him in the side, so he adds, "Don't worry. You're all going to be great. Listen for your name and come over when it's called."

I quickly scan the other contestants' expressions to see if they're as nervous as I am at this moment, and thankfully, every one of them looks uneasy. Everyone but Alex March, that is. He looks like someone just told him he won the damn lottery. No doubt he thinks he's going to outshine us all in this part of the competition too since he's so good looking. I bet the audience is going to love his dark eyes that do that sultry thing they do without him even trying.

K.M. SCOTT

"Don't let this interview thing freak you out. It's just like going for a job, right?"

I turn to see the woman at the next kitchen station smiling at me. Pretty with blond hair and big blue eyes, she looks so sweet that I instantly feel bad that I don't know a thing about her. Frantically, I try to remember her name. Kim? Cam? Damnit! I've been so focused on goddamned Alex March that I can't even recall a single contestant other than him.

"Thanks."

For a long moment, I hesitate in the hopes that she'll fill in the dead space and remind me of her name. Thankfully, she does and spares me the embarrassment of admitting I haven't paid attention to anyone but Mr. Superchef today.

"I'm Emma. And you're Kat, right?"

She extends her hand to give me a handshake, and I smile. "Thanks. Yeah, I'm Kat. I guess I must look pretty worried since you felt like you had to give me a pep talk, huh?"

"It's okay," she says, waving away my concern. "I'm a little freaked about it too. This is the second time I'm doing a reality show like this, so I should be better at it."

"The second time? Really?" I ask, suddenly surprised that someone would be allowed back to compete after losing before.

That gives me some hope that if I don't win Chef on Chef my chance at competing on another one of these shows won't be ruined. God, I've already talked myself into losing. I really need to stop that.

Emma nods like she's embarrassed, so I quickly say, "That makes me feel better because I get the feeling I'm not going to be standing in the winner's circle this round."

So much for trying to think of myself as a winner.

I watch as her gaze moves past me to Alex standing at his station to my right. "I think I know who you believe is the front runner."

Glancing over, I see Alex utterly focused on arranging his knives. God, even when we have down time he's all about the job!

"Well, he does seem to have my favorite dish down pat," I say with far more resentment in my voice than I had hoped would come riding out on each word.

Right before my eyes, I see Emma come under his spell. What the hell does this guy have that makes everyone like him?

"Well, he's exactly like the kind of guy who won in the first competition I was in. Tall, dark, and gorgeous," she says in a dreamy voice.

So much for finding a friend here.

"Looks aren't everything," I say, knowing full well his ability as a chef is fantastic too.

Jesus does Alex March not have a single flaw?

Emma drags her gaze away from him and his fantasticness to give me a smile. "You're right. I had basically given myself not a chance in hell once he walked in, but I need to be thinking like you. Looks aren't everything. If they let us into this competition, then they must think we have something great about us."

"Exactly. So what if he's good looking and great in the kitchen? They aren't looking for a husband. They're looking for a winner, and that can be any one of us, including you or me," I say with far more confidence than I usually possess.

"Thank you!" Emma says, grabbing my hands to give them an enthusiastic squeeze. "That's exactly what I needed to hear after my vegetarian lasagna turned out to be less than wonderful."

Her smile fades to a frown, so I say, "Don't get down. It's still early in the competition, and I bet you're fantastic on camera. You're gorgeous, so that's halfway there, and you know the kinds of questions they're going to ask, so I bet you do incredible when they call your name."

"Emma! You're up!" Shane calls out from the other side of the room.

A look of terror flashes in her eyes. "I guess that's me. Wish me luck."

"You're going to be great. Good luck!"

She hurries off, leaving me standing in front of the oven in my area. Everyone follows her to watch the interview, likely feeling nervous like I do.

Everyone except Alex, of course.

I turn to look over at him and see him still playing

around with his knives. Is he so confident that he doesn't even feel curious about what kinds of questions they're going to ask us?

Just then, he turns his head and smiles at me. Even his teeth are perfect. God, I really do hate him.

"That was nice of you to be so kind to her," he says.

"Eavesdrop much?" I ask, barely containing my loathing for this guy.

"Hard not to when we're all in the same room," he says without a hint of guilt for his bad manners. "Don't worry. You're going to be great just like you told her. Just smile a little every once in a while."

Did this asshole just tell me to smile more? Oh. My. God. He's going to be lucky if I don't use those damn knives of his on him.

"Thanks, but I'm not interested in taking the advice of someone who clearly doesn't have much interest in anyone but himself. Maybe you should try to be focused on someone other than yourself once in a while. People might like you better if you did."

My insult hits home, just as I wanted it to, and for the first time, Alex March looks something less than confident. Good. Maybe that will provide the rest of us a chance.

I don't give him the opportunity to reply to my comment, instead spinning on my heel to go watch Emma do her interview. By the time I join the rest of the group, she's finished answering the first question

Maria asked her and looks perfectly comfortable on the stool she's sitting on in front of the camera.

"Tell me about the first time you walked into a kitchen and knew that's where you wanted to be, Emma."

Oh, that's an easy one for me. The first time I felt that way about cooking was when I was eight and my father brought me to work with him because my mother had to be out of town for the weekend with a client. The moment I walked into his kitchen and saw all that stainless steel surrounding me I knew that's what I wanted to do with my life. I watched my father that day and thought he was a god with how he created such incredible dishes with ease. I wanted to be him but even more, I wanted to be the one standing there in control of that kitchen.

Emma finishes answering that question, and I notice Alex has positioned himself next to me as Maria continues to ask her about things like what she does for fun and what hobbies she has. Emma happily explains how she likes to go wind surfing, and her favorite pastime is to cross stitch because it's so relaxing. Jesus, she sounds like a terrific person.

My mind races with possible answers if they ask me the same questions. I don't do much for fun since I work all the time, and I don't have any hobbies. Damnit! I hope these aren't the standard questions they plan to ask everyone.

By the time she's finished her interview, everyone

knows more about her and cheers her on as she steps away from the camera. I clap, hoping the next name called won't be mine, and when Shane yells out the next contestant to come up for their interview, I cringe.

"Alex, you're up!"

CHAPTER FIVE

lex

I SETTLE IN ON THE WOODEN STOOL THEY'VE provided for the interview and smile at the woman standing next to Maria. I saw her earlier today when I arrived, but I didn't know she was part of the crew working this show.

Too bad there's that clause in the contract that says absolutely no fraternization between the crew and contestants. I would have liked to find out more about her other than she's stunning with long black hair and brown eyes and a great body.

She comes over to stand in front of me and gives me a smile. "Don't worry. You'll be fine. Just be yourself, Alex."

"I feel like I'm at a disadvantage since you know my name and I don't know yours," I say in a low voice as she brushes something off my shoulder.

"Sophia," she says with a smile. "I'm Maria's assistant. Good luck!"

"Thanks, Sophia."

Stunning name for a stunning woman. I watch her walk away, letting my gaze drift down her long legs underneath the floor-length forest green dress she's wearing. I'm nearly six five, and she's got to be over six foot. I like tall women, and she's got everything in all the right places.

A few feet away, the crowd of fellow contestants waits for Maria to begin asking questions, and I swear I hear someone groan as Sophia walks back to her place next to her boss. Turning my head toward them, I see that Kat woman glaring at me.

What the hell is her problem? She acts like I killed one of her family members or something. Does she have me confused with someone else? She must because the handful of times I've been around her I've said nothing to offend her.

"Okay, Alex. Ready for your first question?" Maria asks with a mischievous look in her eyes.

"Ready. Give me your worst. Or your best, depending on how you want this to go," I answer with a chuckle.

She smiles, letting me know she got the joke, and

says, "First question. If you weren't a chef, what would you want to do with your life?"

Christ, talk about coming out of the gate with a tough one. I have to think about that for a few seconds, but it's hard to answer because being a chef is all I've ever wanted to be.

Knowing how important it is to turn on the charm for this kind of thing, I look directly into the camera and flash a confident smile as I say, "To be honest, a chef is the only thing I've ever wanted to be, but I think when I was five I told my parents I wanted to be a forest ranger when I grew up after we spent a week camping at a national park."

That makes everyone laugh, and I know I've succeeded at that first question. Only a half dozen more to go.

"I love the idea of you as a forest ranger," Maria says with a giggle. "You, Yogi Bear, and his little friend. What was his name again?"

Behind her, Sophia says, "Boo-Boo, I think."

I nod, giving her a wink as she smiles at me. Maybe the possibility of being with her isn't hopeless after all. We could hook up after this reality show thing has ended.

"Yes, Boo-Boo!" Maria says, throwing her head back and laughing. "He was the cute little bear. Okay, ready for the next question?"

Giving her another nod, I wait to hear what she wants to know about me now. I listen as she asks what

I like to do to relax, and for a moment, I consider answering honestly.

Then again, mentioning how my favorite thing to do on my days off is lay around in bed with a woman fucking all day might not be what I want to put out there so early in the competition. So I go with something less focused on sex for now.

"What any other young, red-blooded man likes to do in his spare time. Just kick back with my friends having a couple cold ones. I rarely get time off, so when I do, I like to spend it as relaxed as possible."

Not as great as saying I think my days off should be spent in bed between a woman's legs, but knowing my family might end up seeing this interview, I feel like I need to at least pretend I'm an average guy and not someone who would enjoy living out my hedonistic fantasies whenever possible, if I could.

My benign answer charms Maria and everyone else in front of me, and I silently congratulate myself for making the right choice. I'll leave the talk about how I really like to spend my days off until Sophia and I are alone.

The next few questions are about my work at CK, so those go well, except I shorten my answers since I know no one wants to have me talking about my job for the rest of the day. The final question Maria asks involves what I'll do with the million-dollar prize if I win this competition, so I answer truthfully.

"I'll open my own restaurant. It's been my dream

since I was a little boy, well, after my momentary interest in the great outdoors, but it's been my dream nearly all my life to have my own restaurant."

That makes Maria and Sophia smile, and then I'm done with this first interview. I assume there will be more since Cade and Cash have told me reality shows like this routinely rely on breakaway interviews with contestants to give the audience a better feel for who we are. Overall, I think it went well.

"Thank you, Alex. That was great."

I smile and give Sophia another look to let her know I like what I see before getting up from the stool as Maria calls out the next person's name for their interview. My fellow contestants give me nods of approval as I walk through the crowd, all except one.

What the hell is Kat's problem with me?

Since I have to be around this woman for at least the next few weeks, I take the bull by the horns and walk up to her as she stands off to the side away from the group. Her surly expression deepens as I get closer to her, so by the time we're face to face, she looks like she wants to spit in mine.

"I feel like I've offended you somehow, although I can't imagine how," I say, deciding not to go head on with her at first. Better to try the soft touch to begin with and hopefully get her to come around to at least being pleasant.

Tilting her head back to look up into my eyes, this woman with all her five-foot six body at most glares up at me and says, "What offends me is that you think you can charm your way in and out of anything. I bet you flirted with the producer's assistant on your audition too."

Her anger about the way I was acting toward Sophia makes me chuckle. "You think that was flirting? Not a chance. That was just me being me. If I really wanted to turn on the charm, you'd see how real flirting works. By the way, this isn't it."

She narrows her eyes in anger and shakes her head. "This isn't what?" she asks, her words as sharp as her glare.

"Flirting," I answer with a smile I know is pissing her off more than she can handle.

"I wouldn't want it to be, Alex. That's your problem. You think every woman is there to be a plaything for you. I've met your type before. You probably wanted to answer that how you really love to spend your free time is lounging around all day in bed with whatever bimbo crawled in behind you from the club the night before."

Her comment stuns me for a moment, mostly because it's like she's reading my mind, which I know is impossible. When I regain my composure, I take a step toward her, crowding her space to make her uncomfortable.

Turnabout is fair play, isn't it?

"I don't have a problem. In fact, the only person in this building who seems to have a problem is you, Kat.

As for my type, I doubt you've met many men like me."

She doesn't back down. Instead, she puts her hands on her hips and steels herself, staring up at me like she wishes daggers would fly out of her eyes and stab me in the face.

"Why? Because men like you are something special?" she asks, making the word special sound like it's a curse she wants to expel from her mouth.

Jesus, what is this woman's problem with me? We're barely more than strangers, so what's with all the anger?

My ego doesn't give a fuck about the reason why this woman is being so rude. All it wants is to best her in this argument and then go on to best her in this competition.

Looking down at her, I twist my face into a scowl to show my disgust and answer her question. "No. I doubt you've met many men like me because if they're like me, they have no interest in talking to anyone who's so fucking nasty all the time. I have no idea why the hell you're so miserable, but whatever your problem is with me is exactly that. Your problem. So deal with it."

My attack shocks her, and she takes a step back. I wait for her to say something in return since I doubt she's the type of person to not strike back, but she's silent even as she continues to stare at me like she can't believe I had the nerve to talk to her like that.

Sick of dealing with her shit, I turn to walk away but then remember what she said about me flirting my way through my audition. I hadn't planned on telling anyone how I got onto the show, but for this woman, I'll mention it.

Turning back to face her, I say with a healthy heap of smugness, "Oh, and by the way, I didn't have to audition to be on this show. The producers came to my restaurant and asked me. Yeah, that's right. They found me, not the other way around. There. Now you have a reason to hate me. Glad I could help you out with your misery."

I watch with pure pleasure as her mouth drops open in utter shock at the news that unlike her, I didn't have to try out for this competition. Now she can hate me for a valid reason instead of whatever bullshit she thought she held against me.

Kat doesn't have anything to say to that, so I walk away feeling good that she finally got a dose of her own medicine. Whatever her problem is, I don't care. She just needs to stay the hell away from me for the duration of this show or we're going to have words again, and next time I won't be anywhere close to as nice as I was this time.

CHAPTER SIX

at

I WATCH ALEX WALK AWAY AND WISH I WAS ONE OF those people who always had a snappy comeback for shitty men who are convinced they're God's gift to the world. Who the hell does he think he is?

Then again, the fact that he didn't have to audition for this show while people like me did tells the whole story about who he is or at least who the producers think he is. Alex March isn't just some guy who cooks food at a nice restaurant. He's special, and he knows it.

At least now I have a better reason than my jealousy to hate him.

For the next half hour after I get through my interview, I listen to the rest of the contestants have theirs and learn some really interesting things about them. Josie, the youngest one out of all of us at barely nineteen, began dying her hair jet black when she was fifteen because of some superhero character I've never heard of and when she's not working at a restaurant like the rest of us, she plays Dungeons and Dragons. The guy called Murphy is actually named Carter, but he hates his first name and clearly holds it against his parents for choosing that name, if his snide little comments about them are any indication. And Angus with the Scottish accent only lived in Scotland until he was five, but he thinks he got his accent because both his parents have heavy Scottish accents.

These people I like. None of the other contestants flirted with the producer's assistant or acted like he or she was God's gift to the world in every answer. Unlike Alex March, who clearly believes he's special.

"Okay, everyone, that was great!" Shane says to all of us when the final interview is complete. "Let's call it a day. Go home, relax doing all those great things you told us about, and be back here tomorrow for another day of reality television fun. Thanks!"

We all nod and begin talking amongst ourselves as we head back to our places on set. Emma congratulates me on doing so well in my first interview, and I tell her I think she's a master at that because she really was fantastic. I don't know about her cooking skills, but her personality practically radiates out of her when she's talking about her life and that's got to count for something, I'm sure.

"I heard you and Alex going at it," she says in a low voice, as if she's worried I might be angry that she was eavesdropping.

Which is exactly what decent people think when they mention overhearing something.

"He's an ass, and I thought someone should tell him so he doesn't keep walking around like he's Jesus Christ able to walk on water," I say as I pretend to straighten up my station.

"Do you guys know each other outside of this show? You two seem to really have it out for one another."

I shake my head and paste a smile on my face, even though I'd like to give her my honest opinion of him. "No. Well, we met once at a club when his cousin introduced him to my friend. He didn't impress me then either."

Mentioning the fact that my own father raved like some doting parent about Alex's culinary prowess the time we all ate at CK doesn't seem like anything I'd like to include at the moment. I know how it makes me sound. Jealous. Well, Alex March doesn't need my insecurities helping him with Emma.

"Try not to let him get to you. Focus on you because I think you have a real chance of winning this thing, Kat. You're great on camera, and Maria loved your dish today. Don't let your dislike for him cloud your vision here."

I nod, knowing she's right. Whatever that egotistical bastard does or doesn't do on this show has nothing to do with me. I need to remember that.

"Thanks, Emma. I think you've got a terrific chance at winning too. You forget that vegetable lasagna, and I'll forget Alex. Deal?"

"Deal! Now I'm going to go home and watch some trashy TV to relax tonight. See you tomorrow!"

"Bright and early!"

Emma scribbles something on a slip of paper and hands it to me. "This is my number. I thought we could exchange, and if either one of us needs a pep talk and we aren't here, we could call and hear a friendly voice."

I take her number and smile. "That is so sweet. Thank you. Let me get you mine."

When I finish writing out my number, I hand it to her, happy to have a friend here. "Thanks for being so great, Emma."

She waves off my compliment and tucks the slip of paper I gave her into her purse. "We girls need to stick together. I'll see you tomorrow!"

After she leaves, I busy myself fixing everything just the way I like it for the next day, and by the time I finish, I look up to find myself alone in the studio. I really must have been in the zone.

Grabbing my bag, I head toward the door when I

hear Maria call my name. I turn back to see her and Shane standing over near where they conducted the interviews.

"Kat, we'd like to talk to you. Do you have a minute?" he asks.

His voice sounds serious, even if his expression looks relaxed and happy, so immediately my mind turns to what they could want to speak to me about. I give them a smile and walk over to join them, my hands trembling from nerves.

"Sure. What's up?" I ask as they both walk a few feet past where I sat less than an hour ago answering their questions.

They pull up chairs for themselves and Shane pulls one out from under a table for me so we're sitting in a makeshift circle. My brain flashes back to every time teachers got rid of our desks in grade school and we ended up having to do something embarrassing in front of the entire class. God, I hope this won't turn out like that.

Thankfully, Maria jumps right into what's on her mind, and instantly, I feel at ease. "We heard a little of what went on between you and Alex earlier. Is everything okay with you?"

I wave away the idea that anything he could do would bother me and force a chuckle. "Oh that? That was nothing. Just two strong-willed people having a meeting of the minds. Or I guess more correctly, not having a meeting of the minds. But no worries. He and

I are professionals, so I can promise you it won't happen again."

Resentment fills me at the knowledge that they likely didn't stop him before he left today. Why do it with me? They probably think I'm a bitch who's giving their star a hard time.

To my surprise, though, Shane says, "No, in fact, we had no issue with it at all, Kat. Reality TV relies on conflict, and we can assure you that we'll be scripting a lot of it into this show. The fact that you and he have that conflict built in is perfect! We love it!"

"You do?" I ask quietly, sort of confused. Behaving the way we did would be a definite no-no at my job and I suspect Alex's too, even if he is the head chef.

Maria leans forward and taps me gently on the knee. "I thought it was great! Don't think you need to hold back at all either. We can cut out any curses or things like that in editing, so don't worry. He's a big boy. He can handle it. And if he can't, then that's his problem."

I want to jump up and kiss these two people sitting in front of me for giving me carte blanche to tell the almighty Alex March exactly where to go next time. Mr. Special has no idea what he's in for.

"Okay. Thanks! I was worried you were going to tell me you were kicking me off the show because of what happened between us."

"Oh no! No way. As Shane said, reality TV relies on

conflict. We all can agree no one will be tuning in to watch if all we do is make food. Our show is going to have a ton of drama, and you and Alex just made our lives a tiny bit easier since we won't have to script anything for you two. Have at it. That's what shows like this are all about."

The way Maria talks about things, it sounds like they're going to have Alex and me brawling for all the world to see. As much fun as that might be, I don't know if I want to be known for the rest of my life as the woman who fought with the gorgeous chef from the most prestigious restaurant in town.

Then again, what is it they say? There's no such thing as bad publicity? Perhaps people seeing me hold my own against him will mean job offers from better places.

"I don't want you to think I'm being a bitch or anything. I'm sure he's a great guy. He just rubbed me the wrong way," I say, hoping to make them see I'm not really in for a deathmatch with Alex March.

Maria shakes her head and smiles. "We definitely don't think you're a bitch. We like you and Alex, but as we said, shows like this need conflict, so why not take advantage of whatever issue there is between you two? We'll be talking to him about this too, so it won't be like you're some harpy and he's the golden boy. Alex may be the one from the best restaurant in the area, but you bring good stuff to the table, so don't forget that."

"Oh, well, if he's going to be in on it too, let the games begin!"

As soon as I say that, I regret it, even as Shane and Maria beam their happiness at my interest in going balls to the wall with Alex. Then again, if it means I have a better chance at winning this whole thing and taking home that million-dollar prize, I can certainly find it inside me to dish out some more saltiness to anyone who deserves it.

"That's great!" Shane says as he stands, a clear sign our talk is over. "Thanks so much for being such a natural, Kat."

Maria nods her agreement at his assessment that I'm a natural, but all I can wonder is what it means. What am I a natural at?

SADIE SITS IN THE LIVING ROOM EATING A BOWL OF breakfast cereal when I walk into the apartment. Lifting it to show me, she jokes, "Dinner of champions. I guess the truth is out. When you're not around, I eat like a seven-year-old on a Saturday morning."

My mind still distracted by what Shane said and Maria agreed with, I nod and sit down across from her. Did Shane mean I'm a natural bitch? Or worse, was he saying I'm a natural mean girl? Jesus, I don't want people to see me like that.

"So how was the first day? What's the competition

look like?" Sadie asks before shoveling a spoonful of chocolate puffs into her mouth.

I don't answer her question but ask her one of my own. "Am I a bitch?"

My roommate nearly spits out her mouthful of cereal. Choking it down, she wipes the milk running down her chin and answers, "Why would you ask that?"

As I collapse back against the chair, I explain, "The producers said I was a natural after seeing me having an argument with another contestant. I think they mean I'm a natural bitch. Or maybe a shrew. That sounds more like what they were going for. Natural shrew."

Sadie looks at me oddly. "Does anyone use that word anymore? Shrew. It sounds old. I think the only place I've ever heard it was in that Shakespeare play. In fact, I think you're the first person I've ever heard use it outside of that play."

I level my gaze full of disgust on her and shake my head. "You didn't answer the question. Am I a bitch or a shrew or any other word that means a nasty woman?"

She takes a few seconds to answer, which surely means I am a bitch. As I wait for her to say something, a feeling of dread comes over me. God, I am a horrible person just like all my exes said I was. No wonder I'm still single.

"Never mind. Your silence gives me all the answer I need," I say as I stand up to go to my room.

Tonight seems like a perfect time to pull the covers up over my head and hide from the world.

"No, no! Oh, Kat, stop, please," my roommate begs as I begin walking away. "It's not like that."

The problem is that's exactly what it's like. Even my best friend thinks I'm a bitch. Or a shrew. Or whatever other word society uses to describe a woman no one wants to be around because she's awful.

By the time I get to my bedroom, all I want to do is bury myself under my blankets and cry myself to sleep. When did I get this way? I wasn't always so difficult to be with, was I? I mean, I wasn't a three-year-old shrew, was I? That seems unlikely.

While I retrace my life history to find when I became so unhappy, Sadie comes up behind me and wraps her arms around my waist to give me a hug. Against my back, she says, "I'm sorry. I wasn't hedging my bets to find a nicer way to say you're a shrew or a bitch because you aren't. I was just trying to figure out exactly how to say what I feel."

I spin around in her hold and stare at her, wondering how she thinks any of this is helping at this moment. "Just spit it out. It's okay. I'm a bitch, shrew, mean girl, or whatever. It's the truth, so just say it for all the world to hear."

She twists her face into a hard grimace. "I think you're well on your way to wallowing, if you want to know the truth. As for you being any of those delightful things, I don't think so. Yes, you're a strong-willed person who stands up for what she thinks is right. Why is that a bad thing?"

I let out a heavy sigh that feels like it's wanted to come out since I first saw Alex walk into the studio this morning. "It's not, but I don't think that's what the producers meant when they said I'm a natural. That disagreement I got into with one of the contestants was with Alex March."

Sadie's eyes light up at the sound of his name. "The guy from Club X the other night?"

Nodding, I sit down hard on the bed, my shoulders sagging from the weight of my unhappiness about today. "The same. I swear to God, Sadie, I don't know why, but that guy brings out every bad feeling I have inside me. I don't even know him, and I think I hate him. Sounds pretty shrewy to me."

"You are not a shrew. You're just determined and real. That's all."

I roll my eyes at her attempt to make me feel better. "Determined and real. Those sound like euphemisms if I've ever heard one."

She sits down next to me and sighs like I just did. "Okay, then here's the hard truth. You can be difficult at times when you really and truly care about something. You are stubborn and hard-headed, but you have a good heart. I'm not sure what happened today, but don't let yourself get wrapped up in feeling bad about who you are."

Her words march through my brain, and for a few moments, I don't feel so bad anymore. "Thank you. You aren't mad that I got into it with Alex, are you?"

Nudging me in the arm, Sadie laughs. "You can get into it with anyone you want. I admit he has a vibe to him, but if I'm being one hundred percent honest, I really liked the guy who runs Club X the most. There's something about him that works for me."

"You and I both have daddy issues, you know that?"

She elbows me in the side for that comment. "Maybe, but mine are fun and hot. That's the difference."

Isn't that the truth? My daddy issues just make me miserable.

CHAPTER SEVEN

lex

THE BOUNCER AT THE FRONT DOOR OF CLUB X waves me past the line of people waiting to get in, a nice benefit of being related to the owner of the establishment, so I walk into the building to find Cade. A decent crowd has turned out to have a good time tonight, which requires me to push my way through to get to the main bar downstairs.

I scan the people in front of me but don't see him. The gorgeous bartender with the short blond hair and huge rack named Candy or Mandy gives me a smile and reaches out to touch my forearm.

"Hi, Alex. Out to have some fun for a change

tonight?" she asks as the music stops for a brief moment.

Damnit, I wish I could remember her name, but for the life of me no matter how many times she's told me what it is, it never sticks in my brain. I consider just saying whichever one comes out, sure she'll simply hear it and think it's right over the music, but just then I feel a hand land on my shoulder.

Turning to see who it is, I get Cade's face just inches away from my own. "Distracting my people again, Alex? Tandy has work to do," he says with a grin.

Tandy. Damn. I was close at least.

I give her another smile before following my cousin as he walks toward the stairs up to the second floor of the club. It'll be quieter up there so we can talk, thankfully. I need him to explain to me what the hell that whole thing with Kat was today because I can't figure it out.

"Two nights in one week? Dude, you're going to become a regular here if you don't watch yourself," Cade jokes as he walks behind the second-floor bar and I take my place at the end so I can look over the railing to watch the action on the floor below.

"What do you want to drink?" he asks as he begins straightening up the area. "I swear to God I don't know how some of my bartenders work in all of this mess. Fucking lemons and limes all over back here, and the sink is a disaster."

"Something strong. Whiskey. Make it a double. It's been that kind of day," I say as I scan the dance floor.

"See anything you like? You look like you need something to take the edge off. Didn't that reality show thing start today? The way your face looks tells me it wasn't all fun and games."

I roll my eyes at that description of my day. "Try no fun and no games but all bullshit and hassle."

Cade pushes a glass of whiskey in front of me and shakes his head. "The trials and tribulations of Alex March. Next you're going to tell me you hate it."

After I down half the glass of whiskey, I say, "Not exactly hate. Well, not the whole show. Just one person."

My cousin stares at me in disbelief. "You don't hate anyone. I don't think you've ever felt that emotion. Hell, you don't even hate Wilder, and he's the world's biggest pain in the ass. Who is this person who's got you all fucked up?"

"Her name is Kat," I answer before gulping down the rest of my drink. As I push the glass back toward Cade for a refill, I add, "I honestly don't think I've ever met anyone more distasteful in my life."

"Cute name. Sounds like one of the royals," he says with a chuckle as he pours me another glass of whiskey.

"A royal bitch maybe. She's one of the contestants, and I swear to God, man, I'm going to enjoy beating the pants off her in this competition."

Again, he looks surprised by what I'm saying. "What happened to the mellow guy who enjoys life? Where has everyone's favorite hedonist gone to?"

I take a drink of whiskey and let it warm my mouth before swallowing. "I'm still here. I've just added a lust for revenge to my repertoire of emotions. Trust me. This woman has everything coming to her and more."

Leaning toward me, he shakes his head. "I have to know who this woman is. I've never seen you like this."

"You already met her. She was the one with the woman who had a thing for your father last week."

He thinks about that for a few seconds before he gives me a broad smile. "She was pretty nice looking, if I remember correctly. So she's the world's biggest bitch, huh? Too bad. That'll make hooking up with her friend difficult, I guess."

In all of this, I hadn't even thought of that. Damnit, Kat ruined that too. I can't get together with Sadie now. She's probably poisoned her against me after today. Just another reason to hate her.

I finish the rest of my second whiskey and slam the glass down onto the bar. "So much for that. The last thing I need is some angry friend getting in between me and a woman. No thanks. Talk about cock blocking. I swear there isn't a good thing about her. No wonder the other contestants can't stand her either. Well, except for one of them, but I expect her to be gone in the first round since she can't even master a simple vegetarian lasagna."

"Well, what happened? You've got me imagining you two brawling it out over the crème brûlée. Did she make a soufflé of yours fall or something?" he asks with a hearty laugh.

Nice. Now my best friend is busting my ass. Exactly what I need after a day like I had.

"No, asshole. She claims I offend her because I'm charming," I explain, getting irritated about all that happened today once again.

Cade seems confused by my statement, though. "Does she think you should be a classless piece of shit? What's her problem with being charming? I like to think it's gotten me places I would have never gone to in this world without it."

"I have no idea. I guess charm offends her."

My cousin waves his hand like he's dismissing the entire idea of Kat and her being offended. "Fuck her. She's probably just jealous. That's it, I bet. Or maybe she's just doing it for the audience. The people who watch reality shows eat that kind of shit up."

"Maybe the thing about the audience could be it, but it's not like the cameras were on. The show hasn't even started taping. And jealous of what? I'm not some woman with bigger tits or nicer cheekbones. I'm a man. I'm not thinking this is a jealousy thing."

"Jealous of what?" Cade says, his eyes wide like he's stunned I'm not agreeing with him on this point.

"You really are living in some kind of dreamworld, aren't you, Alex? Everyone's jealous of you. They always have been. You're just so used to it that you don't even see it anymore."

What the fuck is he talking about? Everyone's jealous of me? Since when?

"I have no idea what you mean. You aren't jealous of me. My brother isn't jealous of me. Well, maybe you guys are a little since I'm not tied down to one woman and you guys are all but married, but other than that, no. Why would anyone be jealous of me? I go to work, enjoy my life, and leave people the hell alone."

He laughs at my defense. "You really don't get it, do you? Not that I want to feed your ego and make your head big, but you live a pretty fucking great life. You went to school for what you love and then got a job right out of college, not entirely because you're a great chef. I mean, nepotism isn't a bad thing, as you can tell by my job here, but it's not like you had to struggle to find a job and work your way up, dude. You get every woman you want. Hell, I can't remember the last time a woman said no to you. You want for nothing and never have. Whatever you want just comes to you. It's like you're a goddamned magnet for everything great. Success, sex, money—you name it, it's yours. Of course, people are going to be jealous of you."

"You're full of it, Cade. Everything you just said,

except for going to school to be a chef, could be said about you."

He levels his gaze full of judgment on me, clearly disagreeing with my argument. "Okay, tell me if this sounds like anyone. He's the golden boy of his family. Always the favorite. Even the matriarch of the clan loves him best. He can do no wrong in the eyes of his parents. Christ, even his uncles and aunts think he walks on water. Everything goes his way, and no one's surprised because it always has his whole life."

A beautiful woman stops at the bar and smiles at me, so I give her a smile in return before I explain to Cade how full of shit he is. "First off, I can't help it that Grandma likes me best. It's the name. You name someone after her and she's going to like them more than anyone else. Second, my parents and everyone else don't think of me like that. I just benefit from the fact that you, Liam, Wilder, and Cash tend to do things that make them worry. The trick that none of you have ever understood is to not let your family know what you're up to. Trust me. If my mother or anyone in the March clan knew what I do in my spare time, they would be up one side of me and down the other. Since I know that, I don't let them know a damn thing. As for everything going my way, well, I can't help that. It's not like you've spent your entire life suffering, though, Cade, so it seems pretty fucking rich having you tell me all of this."

Another Club X employee interrupts our

conversation with some problem that requires Cade's immediate attention, leaving me alone at the bar with the gorgeous redhead still standing next to me. I have no drink to enjoy, so I turn to face her, happy to pass the time making small talk.

"I'm guessing you and the bartender know each other by what you were saying?" she asks while she reaches her hand out to touch my arm.

"Yeah. He's my cousin. I'm Alex. Alex March," I say with a smile.

The woman moves her hand from my forearm to shake my hand and says, "Nice to meet you, Alex. I'm Kitty."

Kitty. As in pussycat and not that harpy Kat from that damn reality show. Not that I didn't like this woman before finding out her name, but I like her even more now. On top of that, she's not arguing or accusing me of being something I'm not, so Kitty might be my favorite person at this moment.

"Nice to meet you, Kitty. Are you here alone?" I ask, glancing over her shoulder to see if there's someone with her tonight.

She looks past me toward the dance floor downstairs and points toward a woman dancing alone. As beautiful as her friend next to me, she's got long black hair and a smoking hot body just like Kitty.

"I'm here with my friend. Her name is Piper. We saw you when you walked in and hoped to talk to you, but you and your cousin took off to come up here. I figured I'd come up to see if you wanted to hang out and have a good time."

Kitty and Piper, my two new favorite people on the planet.

"I like how you think. What did you have in mind?" I ask, silently thanking God for delivering me two beautiful women tonight.

Leaning in toward me, she touches my shoulder as she says in my ear, "We like to do everything together. If you like, we can all go back to my place."

The delicate scent of her flowery perfume fills my nose as my pulse quickens from her offer. She has no idea how much I like the idea of us all getting together at her place.

When she steps back, I nod, barely able to keep the smile off my face at what's waiting for me in just a little while. "Together sounds like just what I want tonight. Give me a couple minutes and I'll join you two downstairs."

Kitty trails her fingertips down over my bicep to my elbow before giving my forearm a gentle squeeze. Desire dances in her green eyes when she says, "Great! I'll tell Piper. See you in a few, Alex."

As I watch her walk away, Cade jabs me in the left arm with a goddamned swizzle stick. Turning to glare at him, I say, "What's wrong with you? And when the hell did you get back?"

"Right around the time that hot redhead was asking if you're interested in doing her and her friend

K.M. SCOTT

tonight. A threesome? How typically Alex and how perfect considering what we were just talking about."

I look over the railing and see Kitty and Piper staring up at me wearing big smiles. Glancing back at Cade, I chuckle at his insistence that this is typical for me. It's not every night I sleep with two women. That's more of a special occasion kind of thing.

"Jealous much?"

"Not me. Remember, I have the woman I want. But this is exactly why people are jealous of you."

"Cade, after the shitty day I had and then the phone call from the producers telling me they want the bad blood between me and the queen bitch of cooking to continue, I deserve something nice and easy."

"Or two, it seems," he says with a sly grin.

I look down at my two new friends and feel my cock get hard. "Or two."

"So the show wants you to fight with this Kat person? Do they know you're a lover and not a fighter?"

I shrug, unsure what the hell the producers know about me. If they asked around, they'd find out I don't like going toe to toe with people. I don't relish rancor in any form at work or in my personal life, but if it means I can win this competition and get the million dollars, then I'll have to put that aside, at least for a few weeks.

"That doesn't seem to matter to them. They want conflict, so that's what they'll get. For tonight, though,

78

I want nothing but willing women interested in having a good time. Try not to be too jealous of me, Cade."

He shakes his head like I'm doing something wrong sleeping with Kitty and Piper. "No jealousy here, dude. I'm a happy man with the woman of my dreams. Maybe that'll be you someday."

That doesn't warrant a response, so I simply roll my eyes and turn to head down to join my two new favorite people. Tonight isn't about the woman of my dreams. No, tonight is about living out fantasies, and Kitty and Piper can look forward to a good time from me.

A man needs a way to blow off steam, and what's better to forget a bad day than two beautiful women naked beneath me?

CHAPTER EIGHT

at

ON MY WAY ONTO THE SET, MARIA CATCHES ME AND pulls me off to the side in the hallway. She looks thrilled about something, so I hope that bodes well for me.

"I wanted to make sure to tell you that Shane and I spoke to Alex last night, and he's all in on what we talked about yesterday. He actually sounded pretty enthusiastic about it, so I think you two are going to give viewers a great storyline."

Terrific.

"Oh, that's great," I say far less eagerly than I'm sure Alex sounded when he heard we'd be fighting more. "Hey, I was wondering what you and Shane think I'm a natural at. He mentioned me being a natural yesterday at the end of our talk and you agreed, but I wasn't sure what he meant."

Maria taps my shoulder and gives me a big, toothy smile. "Conflict, of course. You're perfect for it. Shows like this run on conflict, so you're going to be great!"

God, that's not what I wanted to hear this morning. Who wants to be around anyone who's perfect at conflict?

"Oh. I guess. Why, though?" I press, needing to hear I'm something more than a bitch or a shrew.

But Maria gives me an answer that only makes me feel worse, not better. "Because you're so serious, and that always makes for great conflict with someone who's so calm and happy-go-lucky."

I can feel my face falling with every syllable that leaves her mouth. "So Alex is happy-go-lucky and I'm serious?"

"Exactly! You're perfect together, the absolute foils of one another, so that makes great conflict. We're all so happy we found this out on day one because it makes our jobs so much easier."

How nice that I made the producers' jobs easier with my serious personality to go up against Mr. Happy Good Times.

"I need to run now, but don't worry, Kat. You two are going to make great TV together!"

As she hurries off, I mumble, "Glad I could help."

Except glad is the last thing I am. Once more, all I

feel is miserable. I don't want to be Alex March's serious foil. He gets to be Good Time Charlie, and I get to be dour-faced and bitchy. Why the hell would I ever be happy about that?

My stomach twists into a tight knot like every time my boss watches me work and then gives promotions to everyone else but me. I had so hoped this reality show would be fun, but now it's the same misery as my regular job. I should just drop out right now and spare myself more heartache.

As I stand there staring at the floor and willing my feet to move toward the door to leave, the man himself walks up to me. So much taller than I am, he naturally looks down on me just because of his height.

When he doesn't say anything for a few moments, it's all I can do to not push him away and run out the door. Instead, I look up into his dark eyes and swear I see pity.

Fuck him. Hating me is one thing. Thinking I'm a bitch or a shrew I can deal with. But pitying me is something I won't let him have.

"What do you want?" I say as sharply as I can.

"You looked unhappy standing here. I thought I'd see if there was anything wrong," he says in a low voice, likely not wanting anyone to hear him being nice to me.

I'm the enemy. He's not supposed to be kind to the likes of me. Where would our beloved conflict go if he did that?

"Nothing's wrong, so just keep moving on."

Something like hurt fills his eyes, momentarily making me wish I didn't snap at him like that. Then he opens his mouth again, and I'm thankful I didn't let myself be nice.

"You know, you don't have to be a bitch every moment of the day. I get what you're doing so you can win this whole thing, but that doesn't have to be who you are when the cameras are off and nobody else is around."

"You think I dislike you for the cameras? Think again, Mr. Happy-Go-Lucky. I dislike you and all people who get everything handed to them. I'd be all smiles too if my life was perfect, but it isn't, so…"

I don't finish that statement because it feels too personal. It makes me feel too vulnerable in front of him.

Thankfully, he doesn't care enough about me or my life to stick around and walks away when another contestant comes toward us. Alone again, I push down my desire to run away and follow them onto the set, determined to win this competition and get the million-dollar prize so I can have my own restaurant all to myself.

When I get to my station, I see Emma ready to begin the day. She gives me a kind smile, and I try to find one for her too. She's the only one who's made an effort to be kind to me so far, so I don't want to alienate her too. I may seem as if I love conflict, but the real me likes when others think well of me.

Then a horrible thought occurs to me. What if the producers decide Emma and I should be enemies like they have with Alex and me? I'd hate it if I had to fight with her just for the sake of conflict on some TV show.

"You okay? You look upset about something," she says quietly as she makes her way over to me.

"I'm fine," I lie, shaking my head as an added way to convince her she's wrong.

But she's not believing me. I am upset. The mere thought of being forced to fight with her to win this competition makes me unhappy, and that little talk Alex and I had out in the hall did nothing to make me feel better about things with him.

"Are you ready to make some cooking magic happen?" she says with a giggle. "That's what the producers on the last show I was on used to say."

Her kindness and attempt to cheer me up make me smile. "Sounds pretty hokey, but right now, hokey might be nice. As for magic, I guess we'll see what they have us do today."

Emma starts to say something about some recipe she tried last night for dinner when across the room Angus barks in his Scottish accent, "Who the fuck has been messing around with my things? One of my fucking knives is missing!"

I turn to look at Emma and see the same horror on her face that I'm feeling at this moment. Touching a chef's knives is a definite no-no. Anyone who's worked for even a single day in a restaurant kitchen knows that.

"Oh my God! Who would do that?" she whispers to me as we inch closer to where everyone has gathered around Angus.

"I don't know, but that's the first thing you learn when you start cooking in a restaurant—no touching other chef's knives," I say as I scan the room to see if I can find anyone with a guilty expression.

Nobody looks the least bit guilty, but then I look over at Alex and see he hasn't made a move to join the rest of us near Angus. How odd. It's like he doesn't give a damn that someone did this to a contestant.

Maybe it was him. That would explain why he looks so disinterested.

Angus stomps around looking for his missing knife near his station, his face growing angrier and redder by the moment. "Whoever it is, give it back right now, or I swear I won't be responsible for what happens if you don't. Fucking around with my knives tells me you're not a goddamned professional. That's for sure."

Shane rushes over to help him, followed by Maria who looks utterly terrified right now. "I'm sure it's here somewhere," he says to her as they help Angus search.

"It shouldn't be anywhere but where I fucking left it!" Angus yells. "If this is how things are going to be on this show, then the gloves are coming off this guy. I promise you that isn't what you want. None of you!"

"Maybe someone came in here overnight to clean or something," Michaela, the contestant who's originally from some tiny town in Idaho, suggests. "Are there cleaning people who do that each night?"

The two producers lift their heads from looking under the counter where Angus's station is to shake their heads. "We told everyone involved not to come onto this set until the show begins," Maria says. "There shouldn't have been anyone here after we left yesterday."

"Then it's one of them!" Angus shouts angrily at the rest of us.

Shane and Maria wanted conflict. Well, it looks like they got it. I'm just not sure they were looking for it to be so full of rage too.

CHAPTER NINE

at

EMMA STEPS CLOSE TO ME AND SAYS IN MY EAR, "This isn't great, Kat. It's one thing to have drama for the audience, but we haven't even begun filming yet."

As we watch the three of them frantically search for the missing knife, I whisper, "Nobody looks guilty, so do you think it's possible it could be one of us? Everyone looks as upset as we are. Well, everyone but Alex over there. Look at him. He looks like he can't even hear Angus freaking out."

We both turn our attention to where Alex stands setting up his area like he's blissfully unaware anything is happening that would make him focus anywhere but on his own damn business. How is it no one else dislikes this guy?

"I don't think it's him," she says, disappointing me. "I know you don't like him, but I don't get a cutthroat vibe from him. Honestly, I get a laid back, no fucks given feel from him."

"Exactly! It's the perfect way to hide that he's a thief."

Just then, Shane calls out, "Found it! It was over near where we were talking to Kat at the end of the day yesterday."

I watch in horror as everyone turns to look at me like the mere mention of my name means I had something to do with Angus's knife going missing. He doesn't wait a moment before asking point blank, "Did you take my knife?"

Shaking my head, I try to keep calm and not lash out, but suddenly, defensiveness fills me. "No. I wouldn't do that. I'm a professional. I'd never touch another chef's knives."

Maria quickly comes to my rescue. "No, no. Kat left before Shane and I did last night, and we locked up on our way out."

Angus grumbles something, and all I can think is everyone here hates me now. I so hoped today would be the start of better things.

"Okay, everyone! Gather round!" Shane announces.

We all make our way over to where he's standing

near the section of the set where we had our interviews yesterday. Maria looks like she's about to burst with excitement, which could be a good thing.

"Today will be meetings all day with each of you. We've written storylines for every contestant, and today you get to find out what they are!" Shane says with more enthusiasm than he usually shows.

Since I already know what my storyline is, I wonder if it's necessary for me to stick around today at all. I want to get my hair cut before taping begins, and I might even spring for a manicure, even though I rarely get my nails done. This competition is a big deal, though, and that calls for some special attention to how I look.

"So when we call your name, come over and be ready for some great stuff!" Maria says with a big smile.

These two sure do enjoy conflict. I don't think I've ever seen people be so happy announcing they've figured out who will be fighting one another.

"Angus, you first," Shane says to him before guiding the Scot over to where the meetings will be held.

As Emma and I make our way back to our stations, she says, "Brace yourself for this today. It could surprise you."

"I doubt they did anything more with me. Shane and Maria told me yesterday that they love the conflict between me and Super Chef over there. They want me to keep it going. To be honest, I just don't know if I can be angry every day."

That makes her laugh, probably because she's like everyone else and believes I'm a natural at conflict. "Try to channel anger from somewhere else in your life and then direct it at him."

Changing the subject, I ask her what's been on my mind for the past couple days and hope since she's had experience on a show like this that she has the answer. "So when does any actual cooking happen here? Other than the one dish they had us make, there hasn't been any mention of actually doing what chefs do. I get that conflict is necessary in a TV show, but aren't people who watch cooking shows looking for the people on them to cook?"

My question makes her laugh once again. "Ordinary cooking shows, yes. Competitions are a completely different animal, though. Everyone wants to see people fight and get into it."

Her answer deflates any hope I had that this show will actually focus on food, which is the reason I became a chef in the first place. Other than the odd feeling of dread I have when I have to deal with my boss at the restaurant, I've never gotten into even an argument in any kitchen since I began working in them. Who has time for all this drama in the real world? I certainly don't.

"Kat! You're up!" Shane calls out from across the room, surprising me.

Emma's eyes light up with excitement. Squeezing my hand, she says, "Good luck! I hope you get a great story!"

Confused since I already have a storyline, I force a smile for her and walk over to where Shane and Maria sit at a table with a single chair on the other side for us contestants. Both producers look like they can't wait to tell me something, but I don't understand because we talked about this already last night.

Before I can ask anything, Maria leans forward and claps her hands together. "I cannot wait for you to hear what we came up with for you. I got the distinct feeling you were worried we were casting you as a villain with the Alex thing, so I just know you'll be happy with this!"

Had they changed their minds about me being the resident shrew on Chef on Chef? For the first time since Alex and I got into it, I look forward to what may happen on this show.

"I came up with this," Maria says proudly. "You and Marco! What do you think?"

Unsure what to say, I have to ask the obvious question. "Marco and me what?"

Shane slaps the table and laughs. "That's what I love most about you, Kat. You are so serious. That's great!"

Still not understanding what's going on, I look at Maria and hope to hear something that makes sense. Thankfully, she sees I don't know what they're talking about, so she says, "You and Marco will have a romantic storyline. Shows like this can't run on conflict alone, so we need to throw some sexiness into the mix. I chose him for you because he's good looking. You two together will look fantastic!"

My mouth drops open in shock, but then a thought occurs to me. At least I won't only be a villain or a bitch on the show. That's something. I'm not exactly sure what she means by us together, though.

I can't help but glance over at where Marco stands at his station checking his phone. He is good looking with sort of scruffy dirty blond hair and blue eyes that make him look like he's come right from the beach. He has a nice body too. In the big scheme of things, Maria could have given me someone much worse.

But will it all be pretend, or are we expected to actually be together?

Leaning forward, I whisper, "Okay. About that. Are you saying we have to be together? Like together together?"

That makes both the producers burst into laughter, which I guess is my answer.

"There's that seriousness again," Shane says. "I love it! But no, you don't have to sleep with him or do anything like that, but you will have to act like you feel something for him."

"Are you happy with what I came up with?" Maria asks, and I can see she really wants me to be pleased with this storyline.

I force a smile and nod. "It's great. Thank you. At least I won't just be the mean girl on the show."

"Exactly! We've already told him about you two, so go have fun!"

I consider asking if we'll ever be cooking anything on this cooking reality show, but I decide not to. I'm beginning to think food and doing anything with it won't be a big part of this competition after all.

On my way over to where Marco stands still looking at his phone, I take a deep breath and try to see this as a positive thing. The audience seeing me as someone a guy like Marco could like can't hurt. It's certainly better than what I thought I'd be cast as before today.

Shane calls the next person over as I reach Marco. He looks up from his phone and gives me a smile that's nothing short of wolfish. He doesn't actually think we're going to hook up, does he?

"Heard the good news, huh? I wasn't sure at first since I heard you and Alex over there go at it the other day and I thought you were a total bitch, but Maria convinced me that it was all an act, so I told her I'm all in on this romance thing with you."

My appreciation for Marco instantly disappears. How nice of him to inform me he thought I was a bitch. Great way to start out a fake relationship.

"Yeah, well, I guess I'm going to be pulling double duty fighting with him and pretending to be involved with you," I say with far less enthusiasm than I think he expects.

"I was thinking while I was checking my messages that we should be obvious right out of the gate with this whole romance thing between us. Lots of PDA. Subtlety isn't really what I'm into anyway, so that will work for me."

As he tells me all this, I can't help but think he's just like my first boyfriend back in high school. Brash, entirely too sure of himself, and basically a tool. The thought of lots of PDA, as he calls what we'll be doing together, makes me cringe, but he doesn't notice because he's returned his focus to his phone.

Nothing like being paired with a self-absorbed jackass. I guess there's no use in bothering to ask him about himself and where he works as a chef. God, I hope he's at least a decent kisser. If he's not, having to pretend to like him will be nothing short of hell.

CHAPTER TEN

lex

Out of the corner of my eye, I see Kat walk over to that guy Marco's station and wonder what that's about. Not that I care at all what she does, but he doesn't seem to be her type. He can't stop looking at his phone or taking selfies with him flexing, and she's got a real man-hating thing going on.

Then again, stranger couples have existed.

Why she thinks this is a place to pick up guys baffles me too, though. Maybe that has something to do with the storyline the producers gave her.

"Alex! You're up!" Shane barks out, so I make my way over there to hear what they've come up for my story on the show.

Even before I sit down in the chair across from them, Maria looks like she can't hold in the news of what I'm going to be doing and who I'll be doing it with. All I want to ask is when we'll be cooking since that's what I'm here for, but with the first words out of her mouth, I realize neither she nor Shane has much interest in that.

"So we put a lot of thought into your story because we want the audience to see your strengths, so listen to this. You are going to be wanting Kat."

Maria's words filter through my brain, but they don't make sense. What does wanting Kat mean in regard to this competition?

"I don't know what you mean."

"That's your romance storyline for the show!" Shane says, as if that explains anything.

"You just told me not a day ago that we're arch enemies and I need to build that up, and now you want me to be in love with her? She's paired up with Marco, if what I just saw is any indication, although that doesn't look too promising. No one is going to believe I want her. Trust me on that."

But nothing I say dissuades them from believing their idea to have me pining away for Kat while she's supposedly with Marco is a great one. "They will," Maria says. "We know this business, Alex, and you can believe us when we say the audience will love this. You two will have conflict, but behind that will be you wanting her. Viewers will totally be rooting for you because they'll see you as a multi-faceted character."

As if I'm not that in real life. And in real life, there's not a chance in hell that I'd ever want a woman like Kat. On her best days, she's a miserable shrew. I don't even want to imagine her worst days. No thanks.

This entire storyline disgusts me, as does the lack of any interest in actually doing any damn cooking on this cooking show. I've held my tongue for the past two days, but now I'm done.

"Tell me, will any of this show involve cooking? You know, the thing that's supposed to bring us all together since we're all chefs?"

A look of confusion settles into both Shane's and Maria's expressions, as if I've asked something utterly foreign to what we're all doing here. She nods and gives me a tiny smile, much less excited than her usual toothy grin.

"Of course. It's just that on this type of show, no one wants to just see you guys cooking food. They want real life stories, and that's what we give them because they sell the show for viewers."

Shane abruptly stands up and walks away without saying a word, leaving Maria and me alone. She leans forward and whispers, "Here's the truth, Alex. We chose you because female viewers are going to love you. I knew it from the first moment I saw you. Trust me. This is going to work out terrifically for you and your future."

Unsure if she just implied that they'd already decided I'd win this silly competition, I ask, "So this has nothing to do with my ability as a chef? I'm here as eye candy?"

"The audience likes to watch good looking people. That's why everyone here is attractive in one way or another. You just happen to be the total package. Trust me, Alex. We're going to make it worth your while."

I shake my head as she continues to talk, done with all of this. Before she finishes, I stand up to leave. "No thanks. I didn't sign up for this nonsense."

Enough is enough. I should have followed my gut in the first place. I knew this was a mistake from the moment I met these people at CK that night. This is what I get for not trusting myself.

AN HOUR LATER, I'VE DRIVEN AROUND GETTING more disgusted by the minute. I should have never let everyone else talk me into doing the show. I'm a chef. I'm not an actor or even someone who pretends very well. Let the rest of those people fight it out for the prize money. My peace of mind is worth more to me than the million-dollar prize.

By three p.m., I'm tired of beating myself up for being stupid and thinking a cooking reality show would actually be about cooking, so I head toward Club X to find Cade. He'll bust my balls about bailing on the show, but at least that will take my mind off being miserable about it.

I walk into the club and see it looks just like it always does in the daytime. It always surprises me how stark it appears when the lights aren't dimmed and the place isn't filled with people having a good time.

Nobody seems to be at work yet, so I call out Cade's name but hear nothing back. He's probably in the office, so I head there.

Stefan sits behind his desk mumbling something at his laptop, but his expression brightens when he sees me. "Alex, what are you doing here?"

"Nice to see you too, Stefan," I joke as I walk into the office.

"You know what I mean. I don't usually see you before the night is well underway. Oh, yeah. You're doing that reality show, so you aren't at the restaurant. How's that going?"

Not wanting to have my entire family know the cooking show turned out to be a total failure, I casually shrug like it's no big deal. If I let Stefan know what happened, then everyone with the last name March and Jackson will know. I don't want to be fielding questions from my parents especially, so better to keep what happened between me and Cade.

"You know how it is."

That's my standard answer whenever anyone in my family asks about anything I don't want to talk about. He accepts it like everyone else always does and nods like he understands.

"I came looking for Cade. Is he late today?"

Stefan shakes his head. "He's off. I'm guessing if you want to find him, try his apartment or the bakery. I believe he told me Hailey had something going on today, but I can't remember what right now. Do you want me to call him and let him know you're here?"

I wave off his offer, not needing to see my friend that badly to interrupt his day with his girlfriend. "No, it's okay. I'll catch up with him sooner or later."

As I turn to leave, Stefan asks, "Is everything okay? You don't seem like your usual self today."

"Oh yeah. I'm fine. Just tired. This reality show stuff is exhausting," I lie.

That's only a half-truth, though. This entire Chef on Chef business has been draining, but mostly I'm not myself because I'm disappointed it turned out so badly.

I drive around for another hour, not wanting to go home but not knowing where to go until I find myself in the parking lot of CK. As I walk into the building, I realize how much I've missed being here doing what I do best.

Cooking. Not acting like I hate or love someone I don't give a damn about. Not dealing with drama and bullshit. Just making food people love.

Before I reach the kitchen, my father sees me and corrals me into his office. "I didn't expect to see you here today, Alex. Are you done for the day with the cooking show? How's that going?"

I debate whether or not to tell him what happened with the show, but he's going to find out soon enough anyway, so when I sit down, I decide to come clean.

"That turned out to not be for me, Dad. Lots of bullshit. Definitely not my style."

His hopeful expression disappears, replaced by one full of disappointment. "Oh, I'm sorry to hear that. I had high expectations for you with that. What happened?"

As much as I believe I have valid reasons for leaving the show, I suspect my father won't agree. While Cassian March isn't exactly the king of drama, he doesn't shy away from it when it happens with other people. I doubt he'd understand how much all of that acting and no focus on actual cooking bothered me.

So I do what I always do with my family. I lie.

"I didn't think it was professional enough to be associated with, especially since my name is attached to this restaurant. I would never want to do anything to tarnish CK's reputation, Dad. I hope you know that."

My father is easy to get around. The mere mention of professionalism is all it takes to escape any real discussion of issues because it's the cornerstone of who he is and what he believes in, not only here at the restaurant but in his personal life too. I learned that early on, so whenever I didn't want to do anything growing up, I just made sure to say it didn't seem professional. Back then, I used words like respectable or proper, but it's all the same idea.

If he or most of the people in the March and Jackson clan knew how little I cared about respectability and proper behavior, they'd know anytime I throw those words out is a smokescreen to avoid talking about an issue. Hell, there was nothing respectable or proper about last night with Kitty and Piper, but like most other things in my life, my family doesn't need to know about that.

"I know, Alex. You've never been anything but a wonderful representative of this restaurant. I'm just disappointed that you didn't find it enjoyable."

"It's okay, Dad. I enjoy my life just fine."

Still, that look of disappointment doesn't leave him, and as we sit there silently, all I can think is I've rarely seen him like this with me before. Cash as the older child got the unhappy look far more than I ever have, and now that I'm experiencing it, I don't like it at all.

"So will you be coming back to work immediately?" my father asks, still in that disapproving tone he's used since I told him I left the show.

"Yeah. Have Kane put me on the schedule for tomorrow."

"Okay. Will do."

The utter lack of joy in his voice hits me squarely

in the chest. Christ, this must be what Cade always says it feels like dealing with Stefan. My father's disappointment in me is the last thing I need today.

"I'm going to head out, Dad. I'll see you later, okay?" I say as I stand up to escape this feeling that I've let my father down.

He gives me a smile, but it's forced. "Okay, son."

Fuck. This day needs to end.

CHAPTER ELEVEN

lex

TWENTY MINUTES LATER, I'M LAID OUT ON MY couch in my living room mindlessly searching through channels to watch something so I can get my thoughts off how miserable my father looked when I told him I left that damn reality show. Why the hell was he so thrilled about me being on that anyway? I should have told him the whole fucking thing was a drama-filled bunch of bullshit that didn't even involve cooking.

Someone knocking at my door rouses me from my thoughts, and as I walk over to see who it is, a horrible idea occurs to me. Did my father call my mother and tell her what happened? The last thing I want to do at this moment is talk to Olivia March about how I failed at a ridiculous reality show.

Before I can answer it, the door flies open and Cade walks through, nearly running straight into me. Full of smiles, he holds up a six pack of beer and announces, "I hear someone in this apartment is looking for a good time!"

"You know I'm always looking for a good time, but right now, I'm looking for something else," I say as he pushes past me to walk into the living room.

"What else is there?" Cade asks in that way he has of making everything about fun.

I collapse back onto the couch and confess what happened today. "I left the reality show. When I told my father, he looked like I'd just said I failed at everything I tried in life and I'm going to have to come back home to live with him and my mother."

Cade twists the cap off a beer and leans over from his chair to hand it to me. "Now you know how every day of my life has felt. Welcome to the party. Nothing like the look of utter disappointment on your father's face to make you feel like an abject fucking failure."

I wrap my fingers around the ice-cold beer bottle and let those words sink into me. An abject fucking failure. Fucking great.

As I down my first few gulps of alcohol, Cade asks, "So what happened? Someone make your pesto sauce go sour? Can that happen? I don't know, but whatever it is, you look like someone shit in your cereal this morning."

"Nice visual. Thanks. What happened is they called me in today to talk about my story, and the whole thing with that other contestant and the conflict they were practically drooling over yesterday wasn't enough. Now they wanted me to fall for her while she's supposed to be with some guy named Marco, who by the way looked like he was all in on their pretend romance, but she'd rather kiss a lizard. I don't have any interest in any of that shit. I agreed to do that show because it had to do with cooking, but other than that one dish they had us make in the beginning, we never even turned on the goddamned burners or made a single thing."

When I finish, Cade shakes his head. "I'm confused. They wanted you and that girl to fight, but then you were supposed to be into her while she and some guy are already together? Were they looking for you two to get into a fight over her or something?"

The way he talks about all of the bullshit they wanted to happen makes it all the more clear that I was right to bail on that stupid show. Taking a drink of beer, I swallow it hard and say, "They aren't really together. At least I don't think they are since I don't think they spoke a word to each other before today. It's all pretend bullshit anyway, so I didn't want any part of it. I told them so and left."

I don't mention to Cade about the fact that the

producers only wanted me on the show as eye candy. My best friend would never let me live that down if he found out. For the rest of my life, he'd bring it up whenever he could to torture me.

"So your time on TV is over. Oh, well. What do you plan to do now?"

I raise my bottle in the air and toast the only thing I've ever loved. "Same as always. I'm going to go back to my kitchen at CK and be happy as Alex, the head chef at the best restaurant in town."

Cade holds his bottle in the air but doesn't join in with my toast to work as the only salvation. "I think this obsession with your job is unhealthy, so I say we go out and celebrate your freedom from the drama llamas on that show."

"Going out doesn't sound like anything I want to do. I think we should stay here and finish this six pack before you have to leave to meet up with Hailey."

I know how this goes since he met the woman of his dreams. He'll stick around until she's done with work, and then he'll go with her. I don't begrudge him his happiness, even as I miss the two of us going out on the town every night in the old days.

A big grin spreads across his face. "I can still live my life like I want, man. Being with Hailey doesn't mean I never hang out."

"She's busy tonight, isn't she?"

A sheepish look comes over his face. "She and Meadow are getting together to make plans for the wedding. She's the maid of honor, so that's her job, I guess."

Meadow getting married. Back when Cade began seeing Hailey, I thought Meadow and I would be a couple. We tried, but we were always too busy. Well, I was always too busy. When we broke it off, I always assumed we'd get back together at some point.

No chance of that now. Yet another example of how I failed at something.

"I guess you're free to babysit your sad best friend then?"

"You won't be sad if I have anything to say about it. We'll go out, hit some places to see what the action is, and before you know it, all this reality show bullshit will be forgotten. And don't worry about your father. Like everyone else in our family, he thinks you walk on water. You just got a little splashed up on you today. That's all. He'll be back to thinking you're the best thing since sliced white bread in no time."

His description of me makes me laugh. "Jealous much?"

"Of the golden boy? Damn straight. Always have been. I'd hate you if you weren't my best friend."

I raise my bottle again at that cheery thought. "Nice to know."

My phone rings, breaking into the start of our good time, and I look down at my cell's screen to see it's Maria. Holding it up for Cade to see, I say, "It's the female producer. I think I'll just let it go to voicemail."

"No way! Answer it. I bet they're going to try to lure you back to the show, and I want to know what they offer. Ask for more money."

"Dude, there was no money, unless I won the prize at the end. Then I'd get a million bucks," I explain.

"No money? Maybe you should let it go to voicemail. Then again, I want to know what they have to say."

Curious too what Maria could want to tell me, I answer it and brace for more nonsense as I put the call on speaker. "Hey, Maria. What's up?"

"Hi Alex. Shane and I are here, and we've been talking. We understand you're unhappy with some things about the show, and we're willing to change things if you'll come back."

"I don't know. It seems like this project isn't about anything I really feel strongly about. I agreed to come on because you said it was a cooking show. It turns out cooking has very little to do with it."

"We get what you're saying, and we think we can work more of what you want into the show. Also, if you really don't want to be involved with a romantic storyline with Kat, we can toss that out too. We'd really like you to come back. You weren't just eye candy. I swear, Alex."

I cringe when she says that, and then I see the amused expression on Cade's face. Fucking great. I'm never going to live this down. He's going to throw it in my face forever, just like a best friend should. I'd do the same to him.

Still, I'm not sure I want to be involved in any more of their reality show nonsense. "I have to think about it, Maria."

"Okay, that's good. Thinking about it is better than no, so that's good. Think about it tonight and let us know tomorrow."

"Fine. I'll call you tomorrow. Thanks."

I barely end the call before Cade starts busting my balls about the eye candy comment. "So she wanted you on the show because you're eye candy? Oh, yeah. That's perfect! Wait until Cash and Liam hear this. They're going to love it!"

So much for salvaging some good out of this day.

"Go ahead. Get it out of your system before we head out. I don't need to hear that all fucking night."

Cade stands up from the chair and laughs. "Out of my system? Dude, you're officially eye candy for the rest of your life. I might actually never call you Alex again from this day. You're Eye Candy March. Or maybe I'll come up with something else. Give me some time. I'll work on it."

Fucking fabulous.

"Well, we might as well go out now. I'm going to need something stronger than beer to think about going back to that damn show."

Cade's eyes open wide in surprise. "You're actually

thinking about going back? I thought you said it was bullshit."

"It is, but I hated seeing my father looking so disappointed in me when he found out I bailed on it. If they include some actual cooking and don't force me to pretend that I like that Kat chick, I might go back."

My cousin takes the empty beer bottle out of my hand and begins walking toward the kitchen. "Oh, the siren song of our fathers' approval. That shit will get you every time. Trust me. I know better than anyone else."

Maybe he's right. All I know is I didn't like feeling like a failure in my father's eyes. I like being the golden boy of the family. I'm not ready to give that up.

CHAPTER TWELVE

at

THE DARKNESS OF THE CLUB SADIE AND I CHOSE for tonight's attempt to drown our sorrows allows me to be my miserable self and not have to force a smile for anyone. I don't think I could muster a true, happy grin for anyone at this point. Thankfully, Sadie knows me for long enough that she understands I just need to muddle through this mood for a little while.

"How's the piña colada? I don't think I've ever seen a drink with that much whipped cream. It's more like a dessert than a drink," she says, pointing at the tower of white foam at the top of my glass.

I turn to look at her drink of vodka and orange juice and wonder how she can stand that. "You know how I am. I'm not really a drinker, so I have to camouflage my attempt at alcoholism with lots of sugary stuff."

She shakes her head at the truth about how terrible a drinker I am. "Yes, I know. You're the same way with coffee. I think you must consume more whipped cream than any other person I've ever known."

"Too bad it's never when it would be fun," I mumble before taking a pull on my straw and getting a mouthful of piña colada.

My friend nudges her elbow into my arm and laughs. "Maybe Marco will be into whipped cream during sex."

All that gets from me is a roll of my eyes and a groan. The last thing I want to do with Marco is anything involving nudity and whipped cream. After the hours I spent with him already, I now know the hardest thing I'm going to have to do for this competition is act like I want him.

What a jackass! When he wasn't trying to put his hands all over my body, he was making suggestions about how I could show the world he was someone I desperately craved. I told him no less than ten times to stop pawing at me, but each time only seemed to encourage him to do it more. The guy is like a horny octopus. I'd bat his hand away from touching my hip only to find the other one grabbing at my other side.

The worst part of it all is I don't think anyone had

to instruct him to actually act that way. Once Maria and Shane told him about our storyline for the show, he was all in, one hundred percent on board with the two of us being entirely consumed by lust for one another.

Pretending to be crazy about him is going to be next to impossible if I'm always having to stop his hands from roaming all over me. I just have to remember that this is all part of the experience. I want to win this competition more than I've ever wanted anything in my life, so if winning means I have to put up with Marco and his sexual harassment to get a million dollars, then that's what I'll do.

It's not that much worse than dealing with my boss on most days, and there's no chance I'll ever make anything close to a million bucks there.

"I don't care what Marco is into regarding anything but especially sex."

"How far do you think you'll have to take this whole wanting him thing for this show?" Sadie asks with a distinct sound of concern in her voice. "I mean, they aren't going to expect you to go out with him on a date or anything, right? This isn't one of those reality shows, is it?"

The mere thought of going out anywhere with Marco sends a chill running down my spine. Maria and Shane said nothing about that, but then again, they never mentioned a romantic storyline when I auditioned for the show.

"Do you know Alex March didn't have to try out to get on Chef on Chef?" I blurt out as the memory of him rubbing that little fact in my face comes rushing back to me.

"Really? How is that possible when you and everyone else had to try out to get on it?"

I shrug, not even sure everyone else had to audition. Maybe only I did. Damn, that makes me feel like shit.

"No idea. I guess he's special. Super Chef to the rescue. Not that any of our cooking abilities matter anyway. This entire production seems to be focused on interpersonal things, which of course, puts me at a disadvantage."

Sadie puts her hand on my forearm and gives it a gentle squeeze. "Don't say that. You're as kind as the next person. You just don't take shit from people. There's nothing wrong with that, so don't go convincing yourself that you aren't nice."

"So far, the only person I really get along with is Emma. I loathe one guy and can't stand the other one because all he wants to do is paw me like some animal. One out of three isn't a good turnout, Sadie."

She gives me a sympathetic smile and sighs. "Well, I like you. I have since the first day we met."

"Thank you. I appreciate you being one of the half dozen people on the planet who doesn't hate me."

Shaking her head, she smiles at my slip into the land of self-pity. "People don't hate you, Kat. They just don't know you. When someone really finds out how you are, they always like you."

I want to mention the dozen or so men I've dated in the past year as evidence against her argument that people like me, but I keep that to myself. Tonight is supposed to be for running away from our problems, and here I am hanging out with them like they're my best friends.

"Enough about the mess this reality show is. Tell me what's going on with work," I say as I take another big sip of my drink.

Sadie tips her glass to her lips and finishes the last of her vodka and orange juice. "My boss thinks I would be perfect to go to the convention with her next month. I think it's in Kansas City or somewhere like that. Why would I want to go there?"

"Is it going to give you a leg up when it comes time for your yearly evaluation?" I ask, my mind flashing back to my last evaluation when Deidre chastised me for not working overtime when Raymond had to leave that one day. Literally one time I couldn't stay to cover someone else's shift and that's all she can focus on.

I guess she needs some justification for why she refuses to give me a promotion.

"Who's to say? My boss already likes me, so I'm not sure traveling to the center of the country when I don't want to is going to be a big deal. What if you come too?"

Sadly, I have to turn down her offer. "There's no

way my boss is going to let me take time off after this show. The only reason she agreed to let me do it is I promised to cover her shifts for an entire week when she goes away."

"You won't have to worry about that," Sadie says with excitement in her eyes. "You'll have a million bucks, so you'll be able to tell Deidre to piss off and come to Kansas City with me."

"From your lips to God's ears. Seriously."

Some guy stands up at the end of the bar and announces he's getting married tomorrow, so the entire place erupts in cheers. Good for him. I hope he's happy. At the rate he's consuming that giant glass of blue drink, he's going to be hungover for his big day, though.

Near him, another man sees someone he knows walk in and throws his arms wide open. "Cade March!"

Recognizing the last name, I turn to look toward the door of the bar to see if it's that guy from Club X, and to my horror, I see none other than Alex March walking right next to him. Jesus! Can I never escape being around this person?

Sadie's already focused on Cade, even though he clearly said he was taken the other night. Elbowing me to get my attention, she leans over and says in my ear, "It's those guys from Club X. Damn, I really like the way they look."

"The one is with someone, and the other one is insufferable. Trust me. Looks aren't everything."

I watch as the group of men welcome Cade and Alex like they're some kind of rockstars, each one shaking their hands or slapping them on the back. With every second that ticks by, I loathe that man more than I thought possible. How the hell does everyone think he's so wonderful?

The bartender comes over to refill Sadie's drink, and I turn away from the action at the end of the bar, disgusted again and wishing I had just stayed home. The last thing I need is to see my nemesis when I'm out trying to forget how bad my day was.

"You know what your problem is with him, Kat? I think you like him."

I level my gaze on Sadie's face and glare at her. "Trust me. I hate him. There's not a single bone in my body that likes him. And do you know why? Because he's a spoiled man who gets everything he wants based on his looks and the fact that his family owns a restaurant. He's never had to work for a damn thing. You can see it written all over his smug face."

Sadie's face twists into a look of horror, but if she thinks that's bad, she's heard nothing yet.

"On top of that, he's the type of guy who would actually tell another human being that he didn't have to audition when everyone else had to. Talk about being a dick. Maybe if he didn't get everything delivered to him on a silver platter, he might realize he should be at least fucking pleasant to others who haven't had it so lucky. God, I hate that! Too bad we all can't be handed a head chef job because Daddy owns the business. I bet he's not even that good. Why would he have to be? Nepotism. I hate it. It's the reason Deidre gets to lord her shit over me, and it's the reason I bet every person who works in that kitchen with the almighty Alex March hates him as much as I do."

By the time I finish, Sadie's practically sucked her lips inside her mouth. I don't know why she's surprised at anything I said. It's not like I've ever been a fan of people getting things they don't deserve. I've been complaining about it at my job for the past year.

"Why are you making that face? Did the bartender make your drink wrong?"

She shifts her gaze to look over my shoulder, guilt filling her expression. I turn around to see Alex standing right behind me with that same look of hurt in his eyes that he had when I told him off at the studio.

"I'll be sure to ask everyone in the kitchen at CK if they hate me when I get back to work," he says with a smile I can tell isn't genuine. "Maybe half, but I can't be that big a dick to have everyone hate me. Then again, knowing my family owns the restaurant might skew the results a bit."

Instantly, I feel like shit. Like the worst person in the world. I had no idea he was standing right there and could hear every word I was saying. Why the hell didn't Sadie give me a sign that he was behind me?

I open my mouth to say something, not sure how to apologize since what I said is absolutely what I feel, but he turns and walks away. I look back at Sadie and see embarrassment written all over her face.

"You should say you're sorry, Kat. I know you don't like him, but nobody deserves to hear someone say all those things like you said."

"The guy rubbed it in my face that he didn't have to audition for the show, Sadie. Now I have to be nice to him?"

"Fine. Don't apologize. He deserved all you said and probably more."

Her words come out all choppy, a sure sign she doesn't mean what she's saying. I didn't intend for him to hear all of that. I was just blowing off steam. I didn't think anyone but Sadie would hear me.

I cover my face with my hands as guilt washes over me. "I really am a horrible person. I don't know why. I don't want to be. It just happens."

Sadie touches my shoulder. "Then just apologize. I'm sure he's right outside. He and Cade just left a few seconds ago."

"Probably because of what I said. God, I was so mean, wasn't I?"

When she doesn't answer, I drop my hands and look over at her. "I'm a mean girl, aren't I? Oh my God! I'm such a bitch."

"I prefer shrew. It has a classier, more elevated feel to it," she says with a smile. "Just go apologize, Kat."

"Okay. I will!"

I hurry across the bar to the front door and walk outside just as I see them drive out of the parking lot. Damnit!

Rushing back inside, I sit down and try to figure out how to make this right. Yes, I can't stand the man, but he didn't deserve to hear me deliver both barrels of my hate for him tonight. Now I have to find a way to apologize, but how?

"What did he say?"

I push my piña colada away that tasted so wonderful before but now is like ash in my mouth. "They were pulling out of the parking lot by the time I got out there. I have to fix this, Sadie."

"Just tell him you're sorry tomorrow when you're both back at the studio."

"No! I have to fix this tonight, or I won't get a second's worth of sleep."

Confusion comes over my roommate's face. "Why? You hate the guy. Why would this make you not be able to sleep?"

It's not impending insomnia that truly makes me want to fix this. It's something far more personal.

"Because I don't want to be a mean girl. For once, I want to be nice. So I need your help."

"Of course. What do you want me to do?"

I reach down and grab her purse off the hook

under the bar. Handing it to her, I say, "I need you to find out where he lives."

As she reaches into her bag to get her phone, her eyes open wide in shock. "Really? You want to just pop over to his place to say you're sorry? I'm not sure that's what nice girls do."

"Just get me the address."

I can always count on Sadie to find out things for me. Back in high school, she became an expert level stalker when she suspected her boyfriend was cheating on her. He was, the pig, but since then, she's been able to find out anything about anyone with just a few searches on her phone. I always joke that she belongs working in the CIA and not as an administrative assistant to some CEO.

While she searches, she asks, "Are you sure about this? You going over to his place could end up being a disaster."

"It'll be fine. I need to do this."

"What if he gets all freaked out and thinks you're stalking him?"

Leaning over to watch her do her magic, I answer, "That would be better than him thinking I'm a horrible shrew."

A minute later, she holds her phone up in front of my face. "Found it!"

Now I just have to go there and make things right.

CHAPTER THIRTEEN

lex

As Cade drives to the next bar we plan to visit tonight, all I can think about is what Kat said about me. Damn, she truly hates me. I don't think I've ever had anyone hate me like this. I honestly don't know what to do about it either.

"What the hell was wrong with staying at Jasper's for a few drinks? I know Tim can be an asshole, but it was his bachelor party," Cade says in frustration, unaware why I wanted to get the hell out of there so quickly.

"It wasn't Tim. Tim was fine. Drunk, but fine. It was that cooking show person. Kat. She and her friend were at the bar."

That's not even close to a real explanation, but I don't know how to go into the actual reason why I needed to get the hell away from that place.

At a stoplight, Cade turns to look at me. "The woman from the show? What the hell do you care if she's at a bar we're at? It's not like you have to hang out with her."

"No, I don't have to hang out with her. That's not it. While you and Tim were talking, I walked over to say hi to Sadie. I got to hear Kat give her real opinion about me."

The light turns green, and he presses his foot to the gas pedal, pushing me back in the passenger seat. "So? What the hell do you care what she thinks of you?"

"I don't. Well, I shouldn't. I guess hearing that I'm the world's biggest dick and she's sure everyone I work with hates me because my father and uncle own the restaurant I work at wasn't exactly what I needed to hear tonight."

"That's what she said? Damn, she is a royal bitch."

"She said a bunch more, but that was the main gist of it. That I got my job as head chef at CK because my family owns the place and everyone there hates me."

A slow smile lifts the corners of his mouth as he takes a corner almost on two wheels. "Oh, so she brought out the nepotism business. Harsh."

"Yeah, fucking harsh, but why do you look like you're enjoying this?"

Cade shrugs as if my bruised ego means nothing to

him. "I'm not. It's just that she's not really far off the mark. Your father and Kane weren't exactly going to let you go work at another restaurant when you graduated from culinary school. Not that I have any issues with nepotism. I'm not exactly suffering from it either. Now that I've accepted that Club X is where I'm meant to be, I'm planning on keeping it once my father decides it's time to pack it in and hang out at the pool working on his tan all day."

Nice. My best friend thinks I only got my job because of my last name.

"For your information, let me remind you that I didn't start out at CK as head chef. Nepotism might be part of it, but remember how I was a sous chef when I first started working at the restaurant? Stop acting like I walked through the door and had the deed to the goddamned place handed to me, for Christ's sake."

"Touchy. Okay, fine. You had to work your way up, and I admit you did work your ass off to get where you are," he says like he's trying to make it up to me.

"I still do. Find me another head chef of any restaurant who peels goddamned vegetables and covers shifts for his coworkers. I care about that fucking business, and not just because it's going to be mine someday when my father and Kane go the way of your father and hang out poolside all fucking day. I work my balls off to make great food because I care that CK is the best restaurant in town. So fuck you and anyone else who thinks my life is easy street because I have the same name as one of the goddamned owners!"

Cade pulls into a parking space in front of a bar we haven't been to since he got together with Hailey. After turning off the engine, he looks over at me and grins. "She really got under your skin, didn't she?"

"I was saying that to you, not her. Maybe you got under my fucking skin. Ever think of that?"

"We've known each other all our lives, Alex. I always get under your skin. This is different, though. She got to you. I'm asking why, though."

My level of interest in talking about Kat tonight is practically non-existent, and that includes with my best friend. Ignoring his question, I open the car door and get out, desperate to find some fun in this night to make me forget the misery that woman has caused me.

My cousin runs up behind me just as we reach the door to The Pretty Dollhouse. A former strip club back in the eighties, the owners decided to keep the name when they reopened the place a few years ago. This was one of the first bars Cade and I came to when we turned twenty-one and is always a good time.

"You didn't answer my question. Why do you give a flying damn what some woman thinks of you? The day she gave you a hard time you slept with two women. You live your life exactly the way you want to. No one tells you what to do. So who gives a fuck about this Kat person?"

I stop right before we walk in and turn to face him.

"I don't care what the hell she thinks about me. What I care about is hearing that I'm nothing but some spoiled fuck who got where he is because of his last name."

"You know that isn't how it happened, so forget her. Let's go in and have a few drinks. You can look for tonight's lucky lady too."

Now that's what I'm talking about. A woman in my bed is the perfect remedy for what ails me.

Or maybe tonight will be another twofer. I'm up for that.

An hour later, Cade is having the time of his life drinking and talking to old friends he hasn't seen in way too long. I, on the other hand, can't seem to shake off my feeling of disgust from Kat's attack. Even the beautiful woman standing next to me trying to get a conversation started isn't doing it.

Fucking woman! She thinks she hates me. She has no idea how much I hate her at this second.

"So what do you do, Alex?"

I paste a smile on my face and answer the woman whose name I think is Carrie. Or maybe it's Shari. I wasn't listening closely enough to catch it when she first told me it.

"That sounds really interesting. I never think about the people behind the food I eat in restaurants. Did you go to culinary school?"

"Yeah, and then I worked my way up from being no one on the line to being head chef."

That comes out far more aggressive than I intended, and I see Carrie or Shari lean back away from me. Now I'm offending perfect strangers who actually want to like me.

"Sorry. I'm having a bad night. It was nice talking to you. Have a good night, okay?"

As I walk over to where Cade is standing with some guy we went to high school with, all I can think of is getting out of this place and back to my condo. He'll probably be pissed since it's not every day he gets a night out, but this isn't working for me tonight.

"Hey, I need to head out."

I wait for him to give me a hard time or at least ask me why, but he doesn't do either of those things. He slaps the guy on the back, says goodbye, and then we're walking toward the door.

By the time we get to the car, I have to ask why he so easily gave up his night out. "Hey, what's up? I thought you'd at least ask me why I don't want to stay here. I thought you liked this place."

Cade smiles and looks over the top of his car at me. "I do. You do too. When you aren't miserable over some woman, that is. The Dollhouse deserves us to be in top form, and you are nothing close to that tonight, so why stay?"

"I thought you'd be pissed since it's your rare night out," I say, hating that I'm such a shitty time tonight.

"Nah. I don't really miss going out all the time. No offense, but I like hanging out with Hailey."

"Sounds like love to me," I say as I open the car door to get in.

He slides in behind the wheel and starts the car. "You know what I think?"

I shake my head. "Are you going to tell me you aren't in love with Hailey? Because if you do, I'm thinking you're full of shit. But go ahead. Tell me what you think."

Cade shakes his head and begins to back out of the parking spot. "Of course, I love her. That's not what I'm talking about. I think this whole thing with Kat is bothering you because you don't hate her. You want to, and I get that because from everything you've told me she's a bitch on wheels, but you don't hate her. In fact, I'm starting to think you're bothered by the fact that she doesn't want you."

"Really, Sigmund? Trying your hand at psychology now? Stick to what you're good at, Cade, and psychoanalyzing people isn't it," I snap.

He puts his foot to the floor and the car takes off down the street as I stare out the passenger side window at the trees on the side of the road as we fly by them. "Have you noticed how touchy you get anytime it comes to this woman? You snap at me, but I think it's because I'm more right than wrong. So the question is will this Kat be the first woman you can't have?"

I consider mentioning the fact that I've wanted women before who haven't wanted me, but I don't need to give Cade any more ammunition tonight. He's already thinking he can figure out what's going on with me. He's wrong, though. The last thing I want in this world is that woman.

What man in his right mind would want a woman who hates him?

CHAPTER FOURTEEN

at

AFTER HALF AN HOUR DEBATING WHETHER OR NOT I
should do this as I paced outside in the parking lot, my
heart races as I stand in front of Alex's front door.
Sadie was right. I shouldn't have come here. She tried
to stop me, but it was no use. I can't let this night end
without making this right.

At the very least I need to tell him I didn't know he
was standing right behind me because if I did, I
wouldn't have said all those horrible things. I may hate
him, but I have manners.

I'll just have to make sure to look sincere when I
apologize.

I lift my hand to knock on the door and take a deep breath in. This will be fine. He'll accept my apology and then I can go on with my life.

God, I really shouldn't do this. So what if he heard what I said? It isn't like he ever thought I liked him. I should really just leave and go home.

"What the hell are you doing here?" a voice sharply asks, and I turn to see Alex walking down the hallway toward me.

So much for him being at home feeling terrible after what I said.

"I...I...I wanted to talk to you."

He grimaces at my vague explanation and pushes past me to get to his doorknob. Unlocking the door, he turns to look at me with such a look of disgust I practically shrink to nothing right there in the hallway.

"Whatever you have to say to me you can say tomorrow when we're at the studio. Good night."

I watch as he slams the door in my face, leaving me standing there in the hallway like some unwanted delivery he hopes someone will take away so he doesn't have to see it again. So much for wanting to be a nice person.

As I begin my walk of shame toward the elevator a few yards away, a feeling of self-loathing comes over me. I should have listened to Sadie when she told me this was a bad idea. She was worried he'd think I was stalking him. He never got past his hatred of me to get to that point.

I deserve every bit of his disgust. I've been nothing but rude to him since that first day, and even though he doesn't know why I'm like this toward him, I can't deny the truth any longer.

Jealousy. That's my problem. I'm jealous of him and have been since that day my parents and I went to his restaurant and my father couldn't say enough wonderful things about the meal he made. My father has never once said anything as glowing to me about a single meal I've made him, yet this guy gets gushing like he's some kind of god in the kitchen.

I jab my fingertip into the down button for the elevator as anger begins to replace sadness inside me. Anger at my father. Anger at Marco for his grabby hand bullshit today. Anger that Maria and Shane have cast me as some kind of mean girl when all I wanted to do was cook some great food and try to win that million-dollar prize.

And anger at Alex March for not being a decent enough person to even let me apologize.

The guy couldn't even let me say my I'm sorry speech without being a dick. Oh, no. This is not how it goes.

My head full of what I truly want to tell him, I storm back down the hallway to his door and pound my fist against it. I'm going to say what I came here to say, and if that means I have to yell it through the door, then so be it.

A second later, he flings the door open and barks, "What? What do you want?"

My mouth drops open in shock as I stare at him standing in front of me in just a pair of black shorts. I had no idea Alex March looked this hot under his clothes. Tattoos cover his chest and shoulders, with one arm covered down to his elbow in a sleeve. Muscles I never would have imagined him having complete the gorgeous image in front of me, including chiseled abs that look like they could be used to wash clothes back in the day.

"Well, what do you want? Are you here to insult me again? Is that what couldn't wait until tomorrow?" he snaps even more angrily than a minute ago.

I shake my head, but somehow all the anger I felt as I marched back here to give him a piece of my mind has disappeared. He looks even more perfect than I thought he was before this moment, and I don't know what to say.

"How did you find me anyway? I guess you're not only rude but a stalker too."

As much as I try, I can't get any words out under his withering stare. Finally, I mumble, "Sadie found you."

Alex scowls at me for a long moment before rolling his eyes. "Okay, great talk."

He begins to close the door in my face, but I stick my foot out to stop him. "Please, I do want to talk to you."

In the tiny opening, he glares out at me. "Fine. Say what you came to say."

"Can I come in? It's sort of impolite to keep someone standing out in your hallway here."

"Kat, you're the queen of impolite, so it seems pretty fitting."

I look into his dark eyes and try to find some shred of kindness in them. I think I see a hint of something, so I push down my hurt feelings from his comment and say in a quiet voice, "Please, Alex. I just want to talk."

For a few moments, it feels like the world stops turning as I hold my breath and wait for him to decide if he wants to let me in or not. I can tell him what I came to say from out here, but I'd rather not have everyone on his floor hear me give my mea culpa.

Finally, he disappears from the opening and the door opens. "Fine. Come in."

Relief washes over me, and I step inside his apartment. Instantly, I'm hit with an incredible aroma of something he's cooking. My mouth begins to water it smells so delicious.

"What are you making? It's nearly midnight," I ask as I follow him down his hallway.

"Just something I felt like cooking," he answers, his words clipped like he resents my being there and my asking him anything.

"It smells wonderful. I'm getting garlic and rosemary and something else I can't place," I say as I sense things aren't going to get better between us anytime soon.

"It's lavender," he says flatly. "In the herbs de Provence."

I thought it could be that, but I was too afraid to say it. God, this man intimidates me. Why does he have to be so perfect in every way?

As I turn the corner to walk into the kitchen behind him, I stop dead, stunned at how gorgeous the room and all the appliances are. All stainless steel and professional grade, they're exactly what I wish I had at my place.

"This room is beautiful," I quietly say as I look around at the Italian inspired design complete with white marble countertops and stone detail around the gas stove.

"I like having a place where I can cook, so I redid this room when I bought the condo. The rest of the place is pretty much the same as it was then, but this kitchen is exactly what I wanted."

"You're so lucky to have this. You really are."

Alex spins around to face me and snaps, "So this is what you came to say? That I'm lucky again? Did it ever occur to you to think things happen because of my hard work?"

His anger hits me like a slap to my face, and I shrink back away from him. "I'm sorry. That's not what I meant. I just meant that I'd love to have a kitchen like this in my apartment. Sadie and I barely have a range and a refrigerator. Our landlord doesn't allow us to change anything in our place without a huge hassle. We wanted to fix up the bathroom because it looked like it was straight out of the nineteen fifties, but he fought us on everything we wanted, so we decided not to change anything more after that."

He doesn't reply to my attempt at conversation, and for a long, uncomfortable moment, we stand there in his gorgeous kitchen like two strangers. Well, one stranger feeling awkward and another giving off a look of pure hatred.

"What did you come here for, Kat? I'm a little busy, so if you can cut to the chase, that would be great."

I know I deserve how difficult he's being right now, but I can't stop myself from feeling hurt at how much he clearly isn't interested in my apology. I just want to make this better, but I keep fucking things up.

So I take a deep breath and look around at the beautiful kitchen Alex has before saying what I came here to say. "I'm sorry. I didn't know you were right behind me at the bar. If I did, I wouldn't have said what I said."

His face remains emotionless as I speak, and then he shrugs when I finish. "It's how you feel. I don't see why you're apologizing."

My defensiveness ratchets up a few notches, but I

try to keep it in check. "Because it wasn't nice and I want to be nice, okay?"

He stares at me, his dark eyes fixed on mine so long that I want to look away, but I don't. "My cousin calls you a royal bitch. Or was it a bitch on wheels?"

His question hangs in the air like some lead balloon between us. I deserve that. I have been a bitch to him.

"I'm trying to make amends here, Alex."

"Who asked you to? Did I demand an apology? This is for you, not me. You want people to think you're a nice person, so you're here to try to convince me that I shouldn't think you're a bitch. Right?"

"I'm sorry that I said those things, and I'm sorry for what I said the other day. I know you won't understand why I said them, but I am sorry."

"Why? Because I've been handed everything in life? Is that why I wouldn't understand why you've been a bitch to me from the moment we met?"

Afraid tears might begin to well in my eyes, I look down at the hardwood floor. "Can you please stop calling me a bitch? And it wasn't from the moment we met."

He takes a step or two toward me and stops so his bare feet are in my line of sight. "Yes, it was. I mentioned to you where I worked when we met at Club X because I found out you worked as a chef and I thought we'd have something in common, and you walked away. Sounds pretty bitchy to me."

Still unwilling to face him, I explain how he's wrong. "No, that wasn't the first time we met. I'm sure you wouldn't remember, but I do. We met last year in the fall."

Alex stands in front of me silent, probably trying to remember meeting me, but he can't. Like at Club X, I got away as fast as I could that night too.

"Kat, I swear I think you're mistaken. You're pretty memorable. I think I'd know if I met you before Club X."

I let out a heavy sigh as I stare at my feet. "It was a Saturday night. My parents were in from New York. We had seven o'clock reservations. My father had the veal, and he said it was the best he'd ever tasted. He loved it so much that he asked to see the chef, and you came out."

"I'm sorry. I don't remember," he says, and all I hear is pity from him.

"He raved about that meal the whole night and into the next day until they flew out to go back home."

"Kat, was I rude that night? Is that why you hate me?" Alex quietly asks.

I feel my emotions begin to unravel inside me, but I can't stop myself from looking up at him now that I'm doing this. Shaking my head, I try to smile at how ridiculous it would be to hate someone for one moment in time over a year ago, but I can't. I know what it must sound like to hear this tiny interaction bothered me so much, but I can't help it.

"You were charming and considerate, and I got up from the table and left before you even got two sentences out of your mouth."

Confusion colors his expression. I guess that's to be expected since I haven't told him the most important part of this story.

The part that hurts the most.

"My father is Andrew Truesdale. He's been the head chef at some of the finest restaurants in New York. I became a chef because of him. The happiest days of my childhood weren't when we went on vacation or swimming with my friends in the pool during the summer. They were when I got to go to the restaurant and see my father work. He didn't let me often, but I loved it. The minute I walked into a kitchen when I was a little girl, I knew what I wanted to do. I wanted to be like my father."

Alex's eyes light up with recognition. "Andrew Truesdale? I had a teacher in culinary school who used to talk about him. He's famous in our business. But I don't remember meeting him."

"My father never tells anyone who he is when he asks to see a chef. He says someone did that to him when he was new in the business and it intimidated him for months, so he wouldn't want to do that to anyone else. He thought you were the best chef he'd come across in years."

I stop for a moment before admitting what bothers

me the most. "The problem is he's never said anything like that to me."

"I'm sorry, Kat. I had no idea."

I feel my eyes fill with tears and turn away, desperate not to fall apart in front of this man. "So you see, it has nothing to do with you, really. That's why I needed to apologize tonight. It's actually a thing where it's not you, it's me."

"I didn't know. I'm sorry."

Wiping under my eyes, I take a deep breath in to steel myself and turn back to face Alex. "So I guess it's not just Sadie who has daddy issues."

That makes him smile, and God, it's like looking at pure perfection. I wish I could hate Alex March because he's so damn perfect, but I can't.

"You're a great chef, Kat. Don't think you aren't."

"How would you know? It's not like this stupid reality show is having us do much cooking at all. Except for that first day, all it's been is nonsense."

"Because you are. Sadie told me you were, and I saw that dish you made the other day. It was great."

"Sadie's sweet, but she wouldn't know great cooking if it bit her in the ass. I came home the other day, and she was eating a bowl of chocolate puffs for dinner. Food is not her thing, oddly enough considering she's my roommate."

Alex looks over toward the oven. "Hang on. I need to check this."

As he looks in on whatever he's making, I think

about how bizarre it is to be standing here in Alex March's chef's kitchen after all that's happened. Everything is my fault, and yet he's willing to even hear me out about my fucked up insecurities.

God, he really is perfect. And I'm a shrew.

CHAPTER FIFTEEN

lex

AFTER I GIVE THE PORK TENDERLOIN A QUICK check, I turn back to Kat and see she's still upset. Jesus, I can't imagine what it would be like if I was forever in competition with one of my parents. That sounds like pure misery.

"It's going to be a while, but you're welcome to stay and have some. It's nothing big. Just porcini pork tenderloin."

She looks at me strangely and asks, "Do you routinely cook in the middle of the night?"

"Sometimes. I had this marinating while Cade and I were out, and I decided to just go ahead and cook it when I got home."

Kat hangs her head and mumbles, "After I insulted you."

"Don't worry about that. Cade says lots of people probably hate me, so I doubt you're alone."

My attempt at humor doesn't cheer her up, so I say, "Why don't we go into the other room and relax? If you want to talk, we can, or we can just watch TV."

She looks up at me and grimaces. "I think I hate TV now that I know how it works behind the scenes."

"I know what you mean. That's why I left the show today."

Her mouth drops open in shock. "You left? Was it because of how awful I've been? Oh, my God. I really am a shrew. Actually, if you left because of me, I think I need to accept I'm a royal bitch. Jesus."

Shaking my head, I offer her a seat at the kitchen table. "It had nothing to do with you or any of the other contestants. I just didn't like what they wanted me to do, and I let them know. Then I walked out."

Kat and I sit down, and she leans toward my side of the table with curiosity filling her expression. "What did they want you to do? I'm sure it couldn't have been as bad as the pretend love I'm supposed to have with Marco, the human octopus."

I can't help but laugh at that description after watching him try to cop a feel more than half a dozen times before I left today. "It wasn't that it was bad. It was that it made no sense."

"What? Did they want you to burn something or

completely forget how to use the broiler? What did they want you to do?"

For a moment, I hesitate to tell her the truth, but then I shrug and say, "They wanted me to want you. Sort of an unrequited love thing. I told them that would make no sense after they just insisted you and I had to be sworn enemies."

A look of sadness comes over her, but she nods like she understands. "Yeah, that would be stupid."

"It's not that it's you. It's just that it didn't work in my mind. Then they told me the show isn't really about cooking at all, so I walked out."

"I'm sorry, Alex. I bet you wouldn't have been so eager to leave the show if I hadn't been so rude to you from the beginning."

"I'm thinking I'm going to go back."

"Still, you didn't deserve that. My problems with you aren't with you at all. I know that, but I let my jealousy get the best of me."

Right before my eyes, Kat blossoms into a different person. One who doesn't seem as defensive as every time before this. I like this person.

"Trying to please your parents can be a hard thing. I know that. I've been lucky as the younger son to parents who didn't think they'd ever be able to have children, but my cousin Cade is a lot like you. He wanted his father's approval for years, and in actuality he had it all along, but he didn't see it. So he always felt like shit. In fact, I bet there were times he hated me for not having to deal with that."

She tries to smile, but it doesn't work. "You know, it usually just sits in the background and doesn't really come up into the light until my father and I are together, but the moment I saw you, all those feelings of inadequacy came rushing back until all I felt was rage. I am sorry, though. You did nothing to deserve all the nastiness I threw your way. You can't help it you're perfect."

I laugh at that ridiculously incorrect assessment of me. "Perfect? You've got to be kidding. Trust me. I'm not perfect. Not by a long shot."

Kat looks at me with pure disbelief. "Please. I know you have mirrors in this condo, Alex. And the fact that the producers of the show came to you while the rest of us had to try out to get on Chef on Chef. And I bet you can think of a million other things if you try hard enough. You're that guy in high school who had everything going for him. Since you didn't die in some tragic accident, something that seems to happen a lot to the golden boys, you get to live a perfect life."

"That's a cheery thought."

She finally smiles, and it lights up her entire face, making her even more beautiful than usual. "I don't make the rules for the chosen ones in this world. I merely know them. You're one of those guys. Ten to one, when you go to your high school reunion in a couple years, every woman there will want you and every guy will want to be you."

I roll my eyes, even as I imagine my graduating class and can't deny I'd like to have that happen if I ever attend one of the reunions. I didn't bother with the five year, but if the ten-year reunion is going to be like Kat is describing, I might be willing to carve out some time.

"Well, since I've let you analyze me, now it's my turn. You aren't exactly a slacker in the looks department, so I'm thinking you know something about people judging you for how beautiful you are."

A pinkish blush colors her cheeks, but she shakes her head like she disagrees with me. "You don't have to be nice. No matter what I look like, my personality chases people away, so no one is hating me for being beautiful. Trust me on that."

"Well, maybe you should show them how sweet you are. I had no idea you were this nice until tonight. Hell, I nearly crushed your foot in the door to get away from you."

The second I finish saying that I see hurt wash over her face, so I quickly add, "Sorry, that came out wrong."

"No, I deserved that. I was rotten from the start, and you had every right not to want to hear what I had to say. Thank you for not crushing my foot in the door, though. I only have two, and I need them both."

I point at her and say, "That right there. You should show people that side of you more."

Kat shakes her head. "I don't know if I can."

"Well, you're doing it right now, and I've been your nemesis since the moment we met. I'm sure you could be really sweet and funny with a perfect stranger," I say with a smile.

The conversation trails off, and as I sit there in silence with Kat in my favorite room in my place, I can't help but realize that I've never been here and simply talked with any woman. If I bring someone back to my place, my goal isn't to talk, and it isn't to cook. It's to fuck, plain and simple.

"I think it's really incredible that you love cooking so much that you created your perfect kitchen, and you actually cook in it. I can't tell you how many people I've worked with in restaurants who never eat at home because they're so sick of the kitchen at work."

Walking over to the refrigerator, I ask her, "Do you want something to drink? I have beer. I might have something else my brother brought over when he was staying here a while back, but I can't promise it will be any good after all this time."

Kat gets up from her seat at the table and walks over to the counter on the other side of the room. "No, I'm good. I should probably go. Are you going to come back to the show? I promise to be my lovely, sweet self if you do."

"Well, I guess I can't say no then. I don't know if they're going to stick with the romantic story of me wanting you, though. Are you okay with that?" I ask, no longer bothered by the idea of having to act like I care about her.

She blushes again, and I can't help but think it's charming. "I'm not sure any woman would say no to two men wanting her, although between you and me, I could do without Marco and his handsy business."

"Then it's settled. I'll go back. I am going to try to make them focus on cooking as much as possible, though."

"Okay. Good. Well, I better go. Thanks for hearing me out."

She hurries out of the kitchen before I have a chance to say another word, and by the time I catch up to her at the front door, she's practically in the hallway. I don't know what I said to make her run off like that. I thought we were getting along.

"Hey, what's wrong? We were having a nice time, and then all of a sudden, it was like I had the plague and you couldn't get away from me fast enough," I ask her as she tries to open the locked door.

When she doesn't answer, I ease myself around her to prevent her from leaving. She won't look at me now either. Instead, my floor seems to interest her more again.

"Kat, what happened? Did I say something to offend you?"

She shakes her head but doesn't look up at me or say anything to answer my questions. It's like the sweet person she became when we finally talked has disappeared. But why?

"I should go," she says, her head still lowered so our gazes can't meet.

"Would you look at me first?"

For a long moment, she doesn't move, but finally, she tilts her head back to look up at me as I asked. Her blue eyes are glassy like crystal blue pools of still water.

"What did I do?"

"Nothing. I have to go. Thanks for being cool about my being an ass."

I give her a smile, and then the next thing I know, her mouth is on mine and I'm on the receiving end of a kiss that takes my breath away. At first, I'm so in shock that I don't kiss her back. My surprise disappears in a few seconds, but it's too late. She's out the door, and I'm standing there watching her run down the hallway toward the elevator.

Smiling, I press my lips together to keep the delicious feeling her kiss gave me going. I can't figure this woman out.

Even worse, I think Cade was right. She has gotten under my skin, and now I know why.

I guess I won't have to pretend to want her for the show now.

CHAPTER SIXTEEN

at

I SHAKE SADIE'S SHOULDER TO WAKE HER, DYING TO tell her about what just happened. Laid out on the couch like usual after falling asleep to some show, she grumbles something about not wanting to wear water wings. She must be dreaming.

"Sadie! Wake up," I whisper hoarsely in her ear. "I need to talk to you."

She turns her head to look at me with an expression of utter confusion. "Is it morning? Do I have to go to work already?"

"No. It's around two. I need you to wake up. I want to talk to you about something."

Her face goes through what appears to be

calisthenics as she comes back to life. Alternating between squinting and wincing like she's in pain, she slowly begins to wake up.

"Two o'clock in the morning? Is the building on fire?" she asks in a groggy voice as she sits up to face me. "Did the Prescotts let their firepit get out of hand again?"

"No, the building isn't on fire. Everything's okay. Well, it's more than okay, and I need to talk to you about it."

She nods, but I know she's nowhere close to being able to understand what I want to tell her yet. I can't give her coffee to wake her up or she'll be up all night and falling asleep at her desk by noon. Maybe water. That might help.

Jumping up, I hurry off to fill a glass with water for her. On my way back to the living room, I look around our kitchen and wish it was as nice as Alex's.

Oh, God. Sadie liked Alex that night. Actually, she liked his uncle twice her age the most, but she seemed to like Alex too. I get it. Those dark eyes and that dark hair of his make for a great look on him. I hope she isn't going to be upset that I kissed him.

Jesus. Oh, God. I kissed him. I closed my eyes, got up on my tippy toes, and pressed my lips against his and kissed him. And it was a great kiss, even though I think I sort of surprised him with it.

Talk about taking the bull by the horns.

I walk back into the living room and find Sadie a

little more cognizant than when I left. Handing her the glass of water, I say, "Here, drink this. It will help you. I think those vodka and orange juices did a number on you."

She takes the glass in her hand and looks up at me like she wants to kill me. "What's doing a number on me is you waking me up in the middle of the night."

Crouching down in front of her, I plead, "Don't be mad at me. Please? I wouldn't wake you up unless it's important."

With a grunt, she nods and takes a sip of water. "Okay, let's do this. Tell me if he was great in bed or not because that's what this is about, isn't it?"

I nearly fall over at hearing that. "No! I didn't sleep with him. And who do you think we're talking about?"

Finally awake, she twists her face into a scowl. "Alex March. Isn't that who you went to see tonight after you left the bar? So you didn't sleep with him?"

"No, I didn't sleep with him. I went there to apologize for being so mean. What made you think I was going to have sex with him tonight, and doesn't that bother you? You did like him at Club X."

"First of all, I liked Stefan March, the owner. Not that Alex and Cade don't have a great look too, but I prefer the OG. Second, and more importantly, why didn't you sleep with him? You obviously are crazy about him."

Sadie takes another sip of water and acts like what

she just said could possibly be true. She must still be groggy to say that.

"I am not crazy about him. That's nuts."

Leveling her stare full of judgment on my face, she rolls her eyes. "Yeah, okay. Then why is it you haven't talked about anyone else on that show but him? Why is it for this entire week, all I've heard about is Alex March. Alex is this. Alex is that. I've known for days. How is it you didn't get the memo?"

I sit back on the floor and shake my head. "No. That's not true. Until tonight, I hated him."

"Yeah, yeah. What is it they say? There's a fine line between love and hate. So if you didn't sleep with him, why are you waking me up in the middle of the night on a day I have to get up for work at seven?"

"Because I kissed him."

My best friend looks at me for a few seconds and then shrugs. "You make it sound like it was all you and he didn't kiss you back."

I look down at the floor covered in old brown carpet to avoid her gaze as I say, "Well, he sort of didn't."

"What? I don't understand. Kissing isn't one of those things you do by yourself, Kat."

"I was standing at his front door getting ready to leave after we'd had a nice talk and gotten a lot of things out in the open. I don't know what came over me, but he was standing there in only a pair of shorts and looking incredible…"

All of a sudden, I stop my train of thought and look up at her. "He's got a banging body and tattoos on his chest and shoulders and down his one arm. I don't remember which arm. I was sort of shocked that he looked so incredible without a shirt on."

"So you stood there in his apartment with that gorgeous man wearing no shirt and looking that good and all you did was kiss him and he didn't kiss you back?" Sadie asks in a tone of utter shock.

"You know how I am. I don't like to make the first move. But he was standing there with me at his front door when I was getting ready to leave, and he looked so good that something snapped in my brain and I leaned in and kissed him. I think he must have been stunned because he didn't kiss me back for a few seconds, but then he did and God it was good!"

Her eyes get wide, and she waits to hear more, but there isn't any more. Well, other than the part about me running down his hallway to the elevator and being too afraid to turn back to look at him.

"And what happened next? Don't leave me hanging here. You woke me up, so spill it. I know you didn't have sex, but something else must have happened, right?"

I shake my head as shame washes over me. I'm a grown woman of twenty-five, and I need to wake up my roommate after merely kissing a guy. Jesus, I am lame. Lame and mean. Not a great combination. No wonder he didn't lift me into his arms and carry me off to bed after I kissed him.

"Nothing else? You kissed him and then what? Bolted out the door?" Sadie asks, saying those words like they're the last thing in the world that could happen.

But that's precisely what happened.

"I left and rushed to the elevator to get away. God, I'm so lame!" I cry and then cover my face with my hands.

Like the terrific friend she is, Sadie gently pats me on the shoulder and says the exact words she knows I need to hear right now. "You aren't lame. You're just old-fashioned. You like the guy to make the first move. So, if we're being honest, you did something really trailblazing for you tonight. You kissed him, not vice versa. That's definitely not lame, honey."

Slowly, I let my hands fall away from my face and look up at her. "I'm not lame? I feel pretty lame. I had a gorgeous man already half naked for me and all I did was talk and kiss him. You would have rocked his world in bed already."

A smile lifts the corners of her mouth, and Sadie lets out a tiny giggle. "I would have, but that's me. You're you, and that's all you can be. So you bolted after kissing him like Cinderella leaving the ball as the clock strikes midnight. She left a glass slipper behind. Did you leave anything with him?"

That makes me smile. Sadie always has a way of

making me see the bright side of life. "No, but he knows where to find me. I'll be seeing him in less than eight hours this morning."

"Well, now that you officially don't hate him, you two can get together."

Reaching out, I take her hand in mine. "Are you sure you aren't angry? I'd hate it if you hated me."

She rolls her eyes but smiles. "I don't hate you. I didn't have a real interest in him. I told you. I liked his uncle's vibe. It's too bad he's married. He and I could have had a good time. I could explore all my daddy issues with him."

I collapse back on to the floor, thrilled and surprised at how this night turned out. "You're too much! I think the two of us should put away our daddy issues for good."

"Well, since I didn't realize I had any until last week, that's going to be easy for me. You, on the other hand, have been toting those things around for a long time. How do you plan to get rid of them?"

Sadie stares down at me expecting an answer, but I don't have one for her. I did something tonight that might go a long way to eliminating my issues, though. By telling Alex the truth of why I disliked him, I at least admitted I have a problem with my father.

That counts for something, right?

Avoiding her question, I sit up and wrap my arms around her shoulders in a big hug. "Thanks for being so great. I was worried you might be angry with me, and I wouldn't have been able to do anything else with him if you were. You know how it is with us."

Gently pushing me away, she holds me by the shoulders and says our motto. "Best friends before men. Always and forever."

"Always."

With a smile, she says, "I'm thinking maybe we should change it to sisters before misters. It's got a catchy sound to it, don't you think?"

Now it's my turn to roll my eyes. "Go back to sleep. I think you need it."

She collapses onto the cushions, smiling as she closes her eyes. "I don't need to be told twice. Good night."

I walk away, leaving Sadie curled up on the couch as I head toward my bedroom. Everything's going to be fine. I kissed Alex, and it was as delicious as I could have ever imagined.

And now the show is going to be great too.

WHEN I ARRIVE AT THE STUDIO, EVERYTHING FEELS different. A good kind of different. I don't feel like the worst person in the world or some kind of natural shrew people instinctively hate. Emma flashes me a big smile and gives me a wave when I walk on the set, but I don't see Alex anywhere.

Did he decide not to come back to the show?

I hurry over to my station to get ready, and Emma whispers, "Did you hear? Your least favorite person left the show yesterday."

Not wanting to let on that I spoke to him, I let my mouth fall open in fake shock. "Are you kidding? No way! The golden boy is gone? Good riddance, right?"

A twinge of guilt pricks at me for talking about Alex that way, but I'm not ready to let anyone know we aren't sworn enemies anymore. Not yet, at least.

"I know! I was totally surprised too. I guess he didn't like something they asked him to do, and he said no way and left."

As the rest of the contestants begin to file onto the set, I whisper to her, "I wonder what it was that they wanted him to do and he refused. Maybe they asked him not to walk on water?"

Chuckling to make my disgust look real, I see a sheepish look come over her. "They wanted him to pretend to like you, Kat. Now don't go thinking there's anything wrong with you because there isn't. I'm sure it's just that a guy like him would never be okay with acting like his feelings weren't returned because of how you feel about him."

Thankful she's so worried about me, I give her a smile and say, "It's okay. I don't think he'd be able to act that well anyway. He's got to have some flaw, so maybe it's that he's a terrible actor."

Emma's eyes light up at my remark. "That's it! I bet that's the problem. He could never imagine in a million years that a woman wouldn't like him, so he can't act like he likes her."

Shane appears in the middle of the room and holds his right hand up. "Attention, everyone! Today we're going to be cooking. I know some of you have wondered if actual cooking would be happening, so since today is our last day before we start filming, Maria and I thought we should fire up those stoves and ovens and get things cooking!"

A rush of relief comes over me. Cooking I can do. Pretending to like Marco enough to let him run his hands all over me or pretending to hate Alex now after last night was going to be next to impossible for me today.

But creating great meals is going to be easy.

"Just one hitch," Shane says. "Each one of you is going to be making a dish someone else wants you to. So Maria will be walking around telling each contestant who their mate is for today, and you'll have to ask them what they want you to make. Since each of you comes from a different background and experiences, this could be a real challenge. Good luck! We'll be watching to see how you do."

I look over at Emma standing behind her station and give her a smile. All I hope is it isn't Marco who will be telling me what to make. No doubt he'll make it sexual, so I'll be forced to create a dish with oysters or something else he thinks is an aphrodisiac.

Just then, out of the corner of my eye I see Alex

walk onto the set and take his place two stations away. He gives me a tiny smile I immediately begin to analyze, but there's no time for wondering what's going to happen next with us right now.

Maria stops in front of me and says, "Kat, you and Alex are working together today. Good luck!"

Before today, I would have dreaded doing anything with him, but now everything's different. I don't want anyone to see that, though, so I instantly screw my face into a grimace.

"Great. Thanks."

She gives me what looks like a sympathetic smile before moving on to the next contestant. I turn to Emma to see her let out a heavy sigh.

"I got Angus. I hope he's in a better mood than he was the other day when someone took his knife. I'm not sure I can handle an angry Scot."

"You're going to be great. I got Mr. Wonderful. He's probably thinking up the hardest dish in the world for me to make," I say, forcing myself to look miserable.

"You can do this. Just remember you got this, okay?" she says in a sweet voice I appreciate, even as I feel sort of guilty for having to lie to her.

"Thanks, and you're going to do terrific with Angus."

She leans over and says in a worried voice, "God, please don't let him ask me to make haggis. I'll barf all over if he does."

That does sound disgusting, but I force a smile for her so she doesn't go into this exercise dreading it. "He hasn't lived in Scotland since he was a kid. He told us all that, right? So I bet he's never even had haggis."

"From your lips to God's ears. Seriously."

I watch her slowly walk toward Angus and turn to glance over at Alex. He flashes me a grin and waves me over, obviously forgetting we're supposed to be mortal enemies. I stop myself from giving him a smile and narrow my eyes to give him an angry glare.

Now we get to see how good my acting skills are.

CHAPTER SEVENTEEN

lex

WHEN KAT GIVES ME ONE OF HER DEATH STARES, I don't understand why she's acting like this after what happened between us last night. Forget the kiss. Not that I want to, but maybe she's regretting that part of our time together. I thought we made a real breakthrough last night with our conversation.

She walks over to my station like it's the worst thing she'll ever have to do and lets out a heavy sigh of what seems like utter disgust. "Well, we better get going on this, I guess."

I don't know what to say, but then she gives me a tiny smile and I understand what's going on. She's pretending to still hate me. Okay, I can work with that.

"Why don't we try not to be one another's nemesis for today, all right?"

That gets me an eyeroll and another tiny smile. "Fine. Whatever. So what do you want me to make?"

Quietly, I whisper, "I brought some of that porcini pork tenderloin for you. It's in my car. It turned out great. You should have stayed to have some."

I don't mean that to be a double entendre, but I wouldn't have had a problem if she stayed last night and we did more than kiss. Kat gives me another little smile and pretends to be angry.

"That's so nice of you. I can't wait to taste it," she says, her tone of voice kind but her face full of hate for me.

"You know, my brain doesn't know how to process someone sounding nice but looking like they want to tear my head off. It's a little confusing."

She looks down at my knives laid out on the countertop and whispers, "I know. It's weird for me too. It's like my mind can't keep things straight. I want to match my voice to my expressions, but if I do that, things will be all off."

I see Maria and Shane watching the two of us, so I tighten my face and curl my lips into a sneer as I ask Kat, "What would you like to make today?"

In her surprise that I'm asking and not ordering her to do what I want, she turns to face me with a pleasant smile on her face. "You want me to choose? I figured you were going to have something in mind."

Shifting my gaze to the left, I say, "We're being watched, so that look on your face now is going to make the producers think we're suddenly best friends. You better glare at me or something."

Suddenly, she barks, "I don't care what you think you are, Alex March. You aren't better than me, so just tell me what the hell you want me to make and be prepared to be impressed!"

Jesus, this bizarre saying things you don't mean and expressions not matching what's being said are going to get us both in trouble. I can't decide if I'm supposed to snap back at her or just keep my mouth shut.

I see Maria and Shane turn their attention to Angus and Emma, giving us a break. Everyone else can't stop staring at us, though, after that outburst of Kat's. They're all looking over at me like they expect me to bark back something nasty at her.

Lowering my head to pretend like I'm looking for something, I say in a low voice, "You know how you said I'm perfect last night and I told you that's absolutely not true. I think we've found something I'm downright terrible at. Acting. All this pretending to be something while I'm actually feeling quite the opposite is giving me a damn headache."

She nods, still with her angry face on but her voice is back to being sweet. "I know. I don't know how long I can keep this up. You better give me something to cook so I can focus on that or I'm going to blow our cover."

"Okay. Let me think of something. What about beef wellington?"

Kat looks up at me with wide eyes. "Wow, you really do want to challenge me. Okay, I can do that. I wasn't thinking of going full tilt with this, but I'll take it, assuming we have a decent cut of beef in that refrigerator of yours."

I hadn't thought of that. We've done so little cooking on this show that I don't know what I have for her to make a dish with.

Turning back to open the refrigerator, I see enough chicken to feed an army, some pork, what I think is veal, but no beef. Strange.

"No beef wellington today, I guess."

Walking over to look into the refrigerator with me, she smiles. "Good. My beef wellington is never as good as I want it to be. What about something with chicken since you have an entire farm worth in here?"

Okay, what to have her make with all this chicken? I think back to a recipe I read a few weeks ago that I wanted to try at the restaurant. That could be good.

"How about bourbon pecan chicken?" I ask as I reach in to grab a pack of chicken.

Beside me, Kat shakes her head. "We don't have

any bourbon. The closest I can get is some wine. That we have."

Frustrated, I think back to the last chicken recipe I remember wanting to make before that one. It's not common, but it might work.

"Okay, chicken bourguignon."

A look of confusion comes over her. "Chicken bourguignon? I've never made that, Alex."

With a smile, I begin rooting around my station for the ingredients. "That makes two of us, but I wanted to try it, so now seems like as good a time as any."

"I've made beef bourguignon, so how hard can this be?" she asks nervously.

As I search for olive oil, I whisper, "You got this. Don't worry. I bet you've made much harder dishes."

She nods and gives me a slight smile. "Thanks. I appreciate that. And you're right. My head chef is a real winner, and she's been riding me since I got that job, so if I can make something great with her breathing down my neck, I'm sure I can do this."

Kat assembles the thyme and bay leaf she needs and turns to look over at me. "I should probably ask what I need for this dish, huh? I'm going on what I'd use for beef, but I'm sure this is different."

With a smile, I nod and begin writing the recipe on a sheet of paper. When I finish, I hand it to her, and she scans it for a second before looking up at me.

"You memorized this entire recipe by heart?" she asks in amazement.

"I may not be able to act, but I have a great memory. With recipes, that is. Other things don't seem to stick as well, but anything with food as soon as I read it, it's in my head."

"Wow. I'm impressed."

She turns back to the refrigerator to look for the bacon and oranges necessary for the dish, and knowing there's no one around, I whisper, "What do you say to coming over to my place tonight so I can impress you with something really great?"

I finish saying that and realize I may have just uttered the cheesiest pick-up line in the history of pick-up lines. Kat stares up at me like she thinks it was pretty damn cheesy too, so I quickly try to clear up the confusion.

"I meant I want to make you dinner. That's what I meant when I said I wanted to impress you with something really great."

Her cheeks turn bright red, but she smiles and says, "Okay. For what it's worth, I wasn't sure what you meant at first."

"I figured by the way you were looking at me like I was some egotistical creep. How does seven sound?"

Kat nods and grabs the bacon from the middle shelf. "Sounds great! Now to get this chicken bourguignon started before people start to wonder if we're even doing anything over here."

As she works on the dish, I scan the room to see how everyone else seems to be doing. All looks pretty calm, although Kat's friend doesn't look so happy with Angus on the other side of the room.

Leaning down, I whisper in her ear, "What's up with Emma? Is she sick today?"

She glances up at them and grimaces. "Oh, God. If he told her to make haggis, she's not going to make it. That was her big fear when she heard she was paired with him."

I can't help but laugh at the thought of him forcing her to prepare haggis. I couldn't do it. I'm sure I could follow the recipe, but I don't think I'd be able to keep my breakfast down.

"Poor thing. I hope it's not that."

Maria pops up from out of nowhere and marches over to where Kat and I stand talking. Arms folded across her chest, she looks upset. Maybe she saw the haggis.

"This is supposed to be a time for cooking, not getting chummy. You two look like you're having too much fun over here. What are you making, Kat?"

"Chicken bourguignon," she answers as she turns to look for something in the refrigerator.

As if someone turned the light off inside her, now she looks as miserable as she always has around me. I know it's an act for the producers, but damn, it's jarring after we were having such a good time.

"Sounds interesting. Alex, why did you choose that?"

"Because we didn't have any bourbon," I say flatly.

K.M. SCOTT

The answer doesn't make sense because she wasn't here for all the discussion we had, but it's all I feel like giving her. Maria shakes her head in confusion, looking first at me and then at Kat. Neither of us offer anything more to help her understand, and I hope she'll move on to another couple of contestants.

But she doesn't. Instead, she watches Kat work for nearly a minute and then asks, "Have you ever made this dish before? You seem to know what you're doing."

As if on cue, Kat scowls and then looks over at me. "He was kind enough to write every detail down. It's on the paper over there."

The sound of her utter unhappiness makes a few contestants stop what they're doing and look over toward us. I know she's acting, but damn, it feels very real.

Maria studies the sheet of paper with the recipe I wrote and then looks up at me. "You wrote this entire recipe from memory. That's impressive, Alex."

I smile and open my mouth to thank her for the compliment, but before I can, Kat grumbles, "So the golden boy can remember a few things for a recipe. Are we supposed to give him a prize now? When is he posing for his statue?"

The producer's eyes open wide at my partner's snide attack on me. She wanted conflict and drama. Well, now she's got it.

I should say something, but I'm not as good at

acting my part as Kat is. Maria gives me one last glance before walking away, leaving us to the assignment they gave us.

Turning away to make it look like I'm not talking to her, I murmur, "Damn, that was a little harsh."

Kat lets out a little chuckle and says under her breath, "I promise I'll be much nicer at dinner."

With a sly smile, I nod and return to pretending that working with her is pure misery. That it's not is the biggest surprise of this entire show for me.

CHAPTER EIGHTEEN

at

STANDING IN FRONT OF ALEX'S DOOR, I TRY TO calm my nerves so I'm not a total mess. I feel as nervous as I did the last time I was here. I just have to remember that turned out great, and this will too.

I close my eyes and take a deep breath in. I'm going to be fine. So he's perfect and gorgeous and everything I find appealing in a man? That doesn't mean he couldn't like someone like me.

Yes, it does. I'm a trainwreck when it comes to interpersonal relationships. It starts with my father and only gets worse from there.

Stop it, Katerina! You're a beautiful woman. At least people say that. You can do this. He's stunning, but that's a good thing. Would you rather he be hideously ugly and horrible like the Elephant Man with a bad attitude?

Another deep breath and I'm ready to knock on the door and get this night going. I look down my body at the black dress Sadie commanded me to wear because it fits in all the right ways and in all the right places and shows no fuzzies or lint. The area near my ankle where I cut myself shaving isn't bleeding anymore, thankfully. Nothing like showing up at a man's apartment with blood rolling down your foot.

I knock once and then again, just in case he didn't hear the first one, and while I wait for him to answer the door, a beautiful woman walks down the hallway toward me wearing a black dress similar to mine. Blond with great cheekbones and a mouth that's so perfect I can't imagine she was born like that, she smiles at me as she passes, but I notice she glances at the door like she knows the person who lives inside.

"Hi," I say, feeling suddenly uncomfortable.

She nods and gives me a tiny hello before continuing on her way. Does she know Alex? Is she an ex of his? She's gorgeous enough to be one of his exes. How many does he have? Do they all look like this beautiful woman who I now notice has legs that go on for miles?

I try to act casually as I take a look at my own legs. Definitely not going on for miles. Maybe inches or a couple feet at most. They're nice legs, though. Toned from all the walking I do at work. But definitely not long like that woman's.

Finally, she disappears into one of the apartments at the other end of the hall just before Alex's door opens to reveal him standing in front of me dressed in jeans and a blue button-down shirt. I'd half expected to see him in shorts, which wouldn't have been a bad thing because he has a great body.

"Hey, you're wearing clothes," I blurt out, instantly starting off this evening with a little self-imposed humiliation. "I just meant that the last time you only had shorts on."

He gives me a big smile that lights up his dark brown eyes and makes him even more gorgeous than usual. "I thought tonight called for some real clothes. You look beautiful, Kat. Come in. Dinner's almost ready."

The moment I step into his apartment, I smell bourbon. As I follow him to the kitchen, I excitedly ask, "Did you make the bourbon pecan chicken I couldn't make today?"

Alex looks back at me and grins. "I had to have it once it got into my head. Bourbon pecan chicken with garlic mashed potatoes, but to start, I have a Greek broccoli salad. Have you ever had it?"

I shake my head as I walk through the doorway into the kitchen. "No, but it sounds delicious. The whole meal sounds incredible. I can't wait to try it! My mouth is watering already."

"Wine or beer? I've got both. Or bourbon. There's still enough left for a drink," he says while I sit down at the table already set for the two of us.

"I'm not much of a drinker," I confess. "Last night I had a piña colada, and I think that was one of the main reasons I ended up standing outside in your hallway."

Alex turns his head to look at me, and in his eyes I see something wicked and sexy I haven't seen before. "I don't have any rum, but I could get some delivered. You know, since it had such a wonderful effect on you last night. I'd like to see what it does for you tonight."

"I'll just take some wine. I should be able to handle that without doing something wild and unpredictable."

When he sets the glass of white wine down in front of me on the table, he looks deep into my eyes and says, "You act like wild and unpredictable would be bad things."

My stomach does a flip that makes it feel like butterflies are scurrying around in my midsection. No wonder people love this guy. He's hot, sexy, and with just a few words, I swear he's close to seducing me already.

I quickly lift the glass to my lips since I don't know what to say. God, I don't want to ruin the mood, but I honestly never have anything clever to say when it comes to men.

Not surprisingly, I'm single.

"Everything okay?"

Remaining quiet and sipping on this pinot grigio would be my best course of action, but it's almost like I can't stop myself from saying something stupid. "I'm trying not to screw this up. I feel like I have a lot to make up for since I've been a royal bitch to you, although I think I'd like to stick with shrew, to be honest. It has a more noble sound to it."

Even that doesn't change his good mood. With a smile, he says, "Shrew always reminds me of Shakespeare. Thinking you want to be tamed?"

A twinge of insecurity bites at me when he says something very close to what Sadie said when I mentioned the word shrew. She should be the one sitting here with him getting ready to eat what will no doubt be a fantastic meal, not me. She's sexy and funny. I'm a shrew.

Or worse, depending on who's doing the describing.

I quickly change the subject before I make a mess of this entire evening. "Everything smells wonderful, Alex. I bet it's going to taste incredible."

Sitting down across the table from me, he gives me a sexy smile. "I hope so. I'm trying to impress you here. I'd hate it if it turned out to be a complete failure."

"I'm sure it won't, and you don't have to work to impress me. I already know how talented you are as a chef."

"You told me you knew you wanted to be a chef

when your father took you to his work when you were a little girl. I've been thinking about that and how similar it is to what happened to me. The only difference is my father and uncle owned the restaurant. I guess that gave me a leg up, but when I was a boy, I didn't think about that. I just knew I loved how shiny everything in the CK kitchen was and how delicious everything smelled every time my father would take me to work with him."

As I watch, Alex seems to take on a glow as he talks about being a chef. Clearly, it's a passion for him. He looks so happy when he talks about cooking. I wonder if I look like that when I talk about my job. I hope I do because it's beautiful to see.

When I don't say anything to keep the conversation going because I'm so entranced by how genuinely thrilled he is about being a chef and how much he always wanted to be one, he stops talking and leans forward to take my hand in his. It's strong and powerful, just like a man in his position's should be.

"I'm probably boring you with all this talk about how much I wanted to be a chef since I was a little boy."

Upset he's taken my silence as disapproval, I smile and shake my head. "No, that's not true at all. I love hearing how people who've found exactly what they want to be in this world and got to achieve it. I've never met anyone else like me who fell in love with food and cooking as a child. Normally when I mention it, I get strange looks, like they can't believe a little girl could ever think of being a chef like I did."

That makes him chuckle, and I'm sure I've never encountered anyone in the world who looks so utterly happy and so sublimely beautiful talking about their job. Now that my jealousy regarding Alex is gone, I can see why people gravitate toward him. His smile lights up his perfectly chiseled face and makes his dark eyes sparkle.

"Enough talk about me. Tell me who you are when you aren't working as a chef, Kat Truesdale."

God, even his voice is pleasing. Deep, it seems to roll over me like silk. I swear there isn't a fault I can find in this man now that I'm looking at him through eyes not clouded over with resentment.

"I wish I could say I'm an exciting person, but all I do is work. That was one of the biggest reasons why I wanted to try out for Chef on Chef. Well, time away from the restaurant and the million dollars. I'd be lying if I didn't mention the prize."

He listens to me as I talk, his eyes intently focused on me as if every word coming out of my mouth is meaningful. "What will you do if you win the million dollars?"

That answer comes as naturally as my being a shrew does to me. "I'll open my own restaurant. I've always dreamed of owning my own place. I'd still work in the kitchen, though. That's where I'm happiest. What about you?"

He shrugs before answering, "I don't know. I already have my own restaurant. I mean, it's my family's, but someday it will be mine since none of my cousins or my brother have any interest in running it. But I'll still cook too when that day comes. I love it too much to give it up to deal with the things my father and uncle handle on a day-to-day basis."

"You're so lucky, Alex. Not lucky like you've gotten everything handed to you. That's not what I mean. You're lucky because you work in a place you love. It's so obvious that you care about your family's restaurant. I wish I felt that way about my workplace."

That makes him sit up straight, and then he says, "You should come work at CK. And not merely as a chef either."

"CK already has a head chef, Alex."

He nods, understanding what I mean. "A head chef who has to deal with planning meals more than making them on too many days. We're going to be down a chef on the line next month when one leaves to get married and move to Miami. You're as good or better than he is, I bet."

"I'm flattered, but you've never really seen me cook, other than my pesto meal that didn't wow Maria and Shane at all compared to yours and today's dish, which I admit turned out pretty well. How do you know I'd be any good at your restaurant?"

Alex has no idea how much I'd love to work at a place like CK. It's the best restaurant in town, but even more, I would be working with someone who loves his job, not like Deidre who seems to love only using her position as a cudgel to beat her underlings into submission.

With a chuckle, he says, "I think that was Maria's way of hitting on me that day, to be honest. My pesto dish was no better than yours. In fact, I think that thing you do with the pine nuts probably makes yours more flavorful."

Most men would look like egotistical asses if they said something like that, but the way Alex mentions Maria's behavior makes it seem like just a natural fact. Of course, she'd be flirting with him and want to hit on him. Why wouldn't any woman?

"Thank you. I learned that from my father," I say, remembering the day he shared his secret with the pine nuts, the first thing he ever shared with me about cooking once I graduated from culinary school.

A timer rings, interrupting my happy memory, and Alex stands up to go to the oven. "It's time for the salad since the chicken is nearly ready. If you want to grab it from the refrigerator, that would be great."

I do as he asks and find a white bowl full of broccoli and sun-dried tomatoes on the middle shelf. The vivid green and red colors make it look delicious, and the scent of lemon and mustard and something sweet fills my nose and makes my mouth water.

As I set the salad down in the middle of the table, I ask, "What's that sweetness in the salad?"

Alex turns his head as he attends to the chicken in the oven and says, "Honey. The recipe gives a choice between that and maple syrup, so I chose honey."

"That's good because I'm not a fan of maple anything, other than on pancakes. I don't know what it is about maple, but it's definitely not one of my favorite flavors. You know what I think it is? My mother used to get these chocolate candy samplers for me for Valentine's Day, and there was always one or two that were filled with maple. I haven't liked it since then."

When he finishes with the entrée that still needs a little more time in the oven, he returns to the table and begins to serve the salad. As he places mine on my plate, he says, "I bet I can change your mind about maple syrup."

Intrigued, I look up to see a sparkle in his eyes. "Oh yeah? How?"

"I'll come up with something. Now give this a taste and tell me what you think."

The way he says that—I'll come up with something—with his voice deep and flowing over me like silk makes an ache form between my legs. This man is the most sensual creature I've ever met. He hides that sensuality in public, but here in his apartment, it's on full display and thrilling me more than I know what to do with.

I take a forkful of broccoli salad in my mouth and immediately taste all the flavors I'd smelled a moment ago. In addition, the tang of the tomatoes melds with the sweetness of the honey and the tartness of the lemon juice and mustard to create an explosion of flavor in my mouth.

"That's delicious, Alex! I don't even like broccoli, but if it always tasted like this, I'd eat it every day."

He beams a smile at my compliment and sits down to enjoy some salad for himself. "You know what I don't usually like? Sun-dried tomatoes. There's something about them I can't stand, but in this salad, they work. Have you hit a red pepper flake yet? This dressing has it all, doesn't it? Sweet, sour, spice, the whole nine yards."

We continue to talk about food and what we like and don't like all the way through dinner. The bourbon pecan chicken turns out to be as wonderful as I imagined it would this morning, and for the first time in my life, I truly enjoy talking about what I do for a living. His enthusiasm for cooking is contagious, and I want to be around it and him.

A buzzing sound interrupts our dinner just before we're finished, and as much as I hate checking my phone, I have to stop the sound so I might as well see who's calling. "Excuse me. I'm sorry, but I can't stand a ringing phone."

He smiles, so I don't feel too rude when I reach into my bag and see it's not Sadie or anyone in my family but Emma. "This is strange. I hope everything's okay."

"What's wrong?"

My phone stops buzzing and then the missed call notification comes up on the screen before I put it back into my purse. "It was Emma from the show. We exchanged numbers just in case either one of us needed a pep talk. She must be feeling bad after what happened with Angus and the haggis today. I'll call her when I get home."

"Can you believe he had her make that? There are Scots who don't know how to make haggis well, and he forced her to do that. No wonder someone took his knife. He's an asshole, and that was a dick move."

"I know! It made her look bad. I thought I had said all the right things when we were all leaving today, but she's probably feeling terrible about the whole thing. Haggis. Gross."

"And here you were probably thinking chicken bourguignon was bad," he says with a look in his eyes that makes me feel like he's undressing me in his mind.

Not that I'd hate that. Not at all.

CHAPTER NINETEEN

lex

We talk about work and the reality show as I clean up the dishes and start the dishwasher, almost like we've been together forever. That's how it feels with Kat—like we're made for one another.

"I didn't make a dessert," I say with a smile.

She gives me a pout, almost as if she's truly disappointed. "Oh. I guess you're not a guy who likes sweet things?"

I lick my lips at what I have planned and shake my head. "No, I do. I just hate making them."

With a nod, she says, "Me too. I'm definitely not a great dessert chef. That's for sure. I just figured with how you look that you avoid sugar and all of that."

"I avoid nothing in life, including sweet things. I just prefer them a different way. Ready to have dessert?"

Kat's face twists into a look of pure confusion. "But I thought you just said you didn't make anything."

As I walk over to take her hand, I chuckle. "I didn't. That doesn't mean we can't end our dinner with something delicious, though."

She still looks unsure about what I mean, but she takes my hand and doesn't protest when I lead her down the hall to my bedroom. Right before I open the door, she quietly says, "Oh, I guess you must think I'm pretty dim at this moment, don't you?"

Turning to look back at her, I smile over my shoulder. "Not at all. Ready?"

"I don't think I've ever had a man ask me if I was ready to walk into his bedroom like it's a thrill ride or a marathon I'm not sure I've trained enough for."

Her comment makes me laugh, and I turn around to kiss her softly on the lips. "You've never had me."

After opening the door, I flick on the light and grab a piece of black silk cloth off my dresser. Kat walks in behind me and stops in the center of the room. Looking around at my very ordinary bedroom with its beige walls and white down comforter covering the bed, she smiles.

"You had me thinking this was going to be some wild sex den or something with the way you were talking there a minute ago."

"Were you expecting something straight out of a brothel?" I ask with a laugh at how cute she is right now.

"No, but you asked me if I was ready, so I didn't know what to expect once you turned the lights on."

I walk behind her and slide my arms around her waist to pull her back against me. In her ear, I whisper, "I keep the décor pretty normal. I save the wild for the actual act."

Kat sighs as she leans against my chest, her head lolling back on my shoulder. "Wild, huh? Okay. Give me your best."

Oh, I intend to.

"I'm going to put this over your eyes," I say as I hold up the black silk in front of her. "Don't be worried. I promise I won't do anything you won't love."

A tiny hint of fear flashes in her eyes. "Promise me, Alex."

As I slide my hands up her sides, grazing her breasts on my way up to her head, I nod. "I promise, Kat. I would never do anything to hurt you or scare you. Trust me."

For a long moment, she looks into my eyes like she's searching for the truth to my claims. She doesn't have to worry. Sex is all about pleasure for me. Frightening her would work against what I want.

She lets out a tiny sigh and nods. "Okay."

While I tie the silk cloth at the back of her head, I

plant soft kisses up and down her neck. "You get to enjoy dessert first. Ready?"

"Mmmm-mmmm."

I take that as a yes and gently turn her around so her back is to the bed. "I'm going to set you down on the bed. Just enjoy yourself."

Easing her back down onto the mattress, I can't help wanting her. She's beautiful in that dress tonight, and I've thought about nothing but this moment all day.

"Alex, I should tell you I've had sex before," Kat says with a giggle.

"Not like this and not with me," I say just before I slide her right shoe off.

I press a tiny kiss to her ankle and hear her softly moan above me. So she's vocal when she's with a man. Good. I like women who make noise.

With each kiss, I inch up her leg to near where her dress sits in the middle of her thighs. She's got great legs, and as much as I could spend far more time worshipping her right one, I've got more work to do, so I crouch down again to take off her left shoe.

Kat reaches out and skims her hands over the top of my head, so I took up and see her pouting. "Something wrong?"

"You were going in the right direction and then you backtracked," she complains in a tone that verges on whining.

It's the cutest thing I've ever seen from her.

"You have two legs. Remember, you told me that the first time you came here?" I say with a smile before kissing her ankle.

"Feet," she corrects me and then moans. "Whatever you're doing, don't stop."

I lift my mouth from her calf and shrug, even though I know she can't see it. "Just worshipping your gorgeous legs."

By the time I reach the middle of her thigh on this leg, she's wriggling underneath my hold. "Alex, did I ever mention how much I hate teasing?"

Sliding my palms up over her thighs until I reach her panties, I chuckle. "It's only teasing if the other person doesn't plan to follow through. Trust me, I'll follow through."

"It's teasing if you make someone want something but you won't give it to them right now," she says, this time very much whining.

I hook my thumbs through her panties and gently tug them down her legs. "So impatient."

"I am, and you're driving me crazy here," Kat says, reaching for my arms.

"Do I have to tie you up?" I ask in my best serious voice.

She falls completely still and says nothing for a long time as I watch her. She's trying to figure out if she should be frightened.

But then she surprises me and smiles as she sweetly says, "I'm not against that idea."

Oh, she's got a little kinkiness to her. Good. I like that too.

"Maybe next time. Tonight, I want your arms and legs free. Now no more complaining. Good girls get what they want if they're patient. Are you going to be patient, Kat?"

I get a tiny frown in response to my question. "That's unfortunately a virtue I don't possess, so probably no."

Against her skin, I mumble, "Kat is not a good girl. Hmmm..."

At that moment, I slide her dress up to her waist and get my first glimpse at that gorgeous spot between her legs. As much as I want to have the willpower to tease her a little more, her pussy is too tempting. I dip my head and run my tongue up the length of her slit, stopping when I reach her clit to give it a tiny suck between my lips.

Kat spreads her legs wide, giving me all of her to feast on with my mouth. She's wet and open, and my tongue laps at her juices like a parched man being offered the finest wine.

"Alex, oh...don't stop whatever you're doing there," she moans in a needy voice above me.

I flick my tongue over her clit again and gently suck it between my lips once more. She lifts her hips off the bed and presses her palm to the top of my head as she says, "Oh, God..."

Feeling she's close, I slide one finger into her

drenched pussy and feel her body contract around it. I'd planned on doing far more since I haven't even gotten the whipped cream and honey out yet, but she comes hard against my mouth, and I ride her release, her thighs quivering against the sides of my head as she whimpers above me.

When the tremors from her orgasm finally subside, I lift my head and smile at how perfect she looks lying there still wearing the black silk blindfold. No matter what she wants to say, she's a good girl.

Now's she's my good girl, at least for tonight.

I quickly strip out of my clothes and sit her up to pull off her dress. She claws at my body to pull me to her, blinded to what I look like now because of the black silk over her eyes. Her fingernails gently scrape across my chest, exciting me and making me want her even more.

Easing up her body, I nudge her legs open with my knee and slide my finger through her folds to make sure she's ready. Wet and needy, she tilts her hips up when I touch her clit.

My mouth finds hers just as willing as the rest of her, and I kiss her hard, unable to temper my desire any longer. Kat wraps her arms around me, holding me close as we kiss like our lips hold the very breath we need to live. Her tongue glides over mine, teasing me so I'm rock hard. I suck on her tongue, remembering how incredible she tasted when I went down on her.

I want to feel her cunt tighten around my cock when I fuck her so fully that her body surrenders to me completely. Pulling my hips back, I thrust once, filling her. Kat lets out a gasp when I'm balls deep inside her, and in my ear, she moans, "Please, no more teasing, Alex. Fuck me."

Burying my hand in her hair, I tighten my fist around the silky brown strands and begin to fuck her in earnest. Some nights call for slow and easy, while others call for hours of teasing before I give in. Tonight, though, she wants to be fucked, so it's fast and hard for her.

Her heels press into the small of my back with every thrust into her as her hips match mine in tempo and rhythm. Our bodies meld into a perfect combination of ebb and flow, almost as if we're meant to be. Surprise fills me as I realize I've never felt like this with any woman before Kat. It's like she's my match in every way.

"Oh, God…don't stop…" she moans in my ear, her fingernails tearing across the tops of my shoulders as I pound into her like a man possessed.

I want to fill her with everything I have. I want to hear her cry out as her release tears through her, an orgasm I give her. I want her begging for more of my cock as much as I want more of her perfect cunt.

"God, you feel like fucking heaven," I murmur.

"Mmmm…roll me over. I want to be on top for a while," she says with a smile.

I do as she wants, and the vision of her straddling my hips with my cock deep inside her and that blindfold shielding her eyes makes me think she's too perfect to be real. I set my hands on her waist, but Kat takes over, rolling her hips and taking me even deeper inside her than before.

"Nice trick."

She gives me a beautiful smile before repeating the movement. "Just something I learned in a book once. I've never tried it until right now, though."

Kat sets her palms on my chest to steady herself and begins to go to town on my cock, riding me like she knows exactly what will get me to come. Needing to see her eyes, I reach up to slide the blindfold off her head, tossing it behind me onto the pillows.

She slides down my cock and stills before smiling at me. "I was wondering when I'd get to actually see you during this."

I spread my arms out to the sides and grin. "Do you like what you see?"

Leaning down, she whispers against my lips, "Very much."

Cupping her breasts, I pinch her nipples and nip at her bottom lip. "Same. You keep doing whatever that is you're doing when you roll your hips like that and I'm going to come much faster than I want to."

Suddenly, she sits up and does exactly what I just said was going to make me come. "Good. I'm one ahead of you, so you need to catch up."

Turnabout is fair play, so I stroke my finger over her clit and see her eyes get wide. "You think I'm going to come without making you come again so you're still one ahead of me? No way."

It's rare that I feel this comfortable with a woman, but something about Kat makes me feel like we've been together like this before. It's a good feeling, like when you watch your favorite movie and still live for every great part, even though you know the story like the back of your hand.

I watch her ride me, and with every time she takes all of me into her beautiful cunt, I get closer and closer. She looks like a goddess on top of me, and I know she's close because I feel her walls start to tighten around me.

"That's it, baby. Let yourself go."

Her eyes fill with the haze of ecstasy, and a moment later, she sits down hard on my hips before falling still as she collapses on my chest. Her pussy milks my cock, sending me over the edge a few seconds later. I tighten my hand around her hair, pulling hard as I fill her with all I have.

I don't know how long we stay like that, but when she rolls off me onto the bed, all I know is I miss having her body on mine.

"God, my hips are killing me, but that was worth the pain," she says quietly.

Rolling over to face her, I nod my agreement about how incredible our first time together was. "I'm guessing now isn't the time to say I'm ready for round two then."

With a wicked smile, she giggles. "I didn't say I was tired. Just that my hips ache. That means next round is going to have to be you doing more of the work. You up for it?"

I slide my arm around her to pull her body to mine, loving the feel of her pressed against me. "Definitely. I'll take care of everything. You just sit back and enjoy. Just one question. Which should I start with, whipped cream or honey?"

Kat licks her lips and smiles. "Whipped cream."

"That was my idea too. I think I have a new favorite dessert. I'm calling it Kat à la cream."

She looks at me oddly and then asks, "Where do you plan to put all that whipped cream?"

"All over. Be right back."

I trot out to the kitchen to get the can of whipped cream I bought on the way home and spy a bottle of maraschino cherries right next to it. I've never included them in sex before, but I'm up for it. I grab the jar of honey from the cabinet to add to the fun and head back to my bedroom to find Kat waiting for me.

"Your comforter is going to be a mess after all of that," she says when she realizes all of what's in my hands.

As I come around the bed to set the three containers on my nightstand, I smile. "That's what they make washing machines for. Worst comes to worst, I'll just get a new one."

I turn to face Kat and see her studying me. "What's up?"

"You are the sexiest man I've ever met. It's as if sensuality oozes out of you. I think at first I saw it as confidence, or more correctly, as cockiness, but it's not that. It's that you truly enjoy things."

The way she says that makes it sound like she admires me for the trait that's always been a part of me. "I'm guessing you think that's a good thing."

"It is. I wish I was like that, to be honest."

Grabbing the can of whipped cream, I shoot some into my mouth and smile before leaning down to kiss her. Her tongue laps the treat off my lips before she giggles.

"See? You're every bit as sensual as I am. You just needed to be with someone who brings that out in you," I whisper against her lips.

Kat sighs and then bites her lower lip. "Maybe. Or maybe I just wish I was."

I press down on the whipped cream nozzle and paint a line of white down between her breasts. "Stick with me. I'll tease out all that sensuality I know you have inside. Now lay back and let me play."

She does as I order, leaning back on the pile of pillows near the head of the bed. Looking up at me, she smiles, and I can't remember anyone ever looking so beautiful.

"I feel like some kind of human smorgasbord."

Dipping my head, I flick my tongue over her skin, lapping up the cream as I stare up at her and she watches me. "Wait until the honey and cherries join in."

My cock feels like it's made of steel I'm so hard, but I need to wait before I plunge into her body again. I want to worship every inch of her first.

"Hand me the honey."

As I cover her left nipple in cream, she holds the pot of honey with the dipper above my head. Looking up at her, I smile. "You look like you're about to pour that over my head. Anything that gets on me you have to lick off."

My tongue dances against her hard nipple before I suck off the sweetness from the whipped cream on her skin. Kat moans softly until I gently bite down on her tender skin when she lets out a tiny yelp.

Lifting my head, I search her face to see if that really hurt, but she's all smiles. "I was worried I might have bitten down too hard."

She shakes her head as her smile grows bigger. "Nope. Just a little surprised. That's all."

I lean forward and kiss that beautiful mouth of hers. "Good because I plan on devouring every inch of you. Time for the honey."

When I sit back on my heels, I hold the jar of honey up and raise the dipper a few inches above the rim. Kat watches intently, like she's enthralled by my every move and curious about what's going to happen next.

"I want to eat this off your gorgeous tits," I say as I drizzle the golden treat over her right breast. "Ready?"

She licks her lips and nods before she sighs ever so quietly. "I don't think I've ever been this aroused by food before. I swear I'm going to have to hold back from coming the moment your mouth touches me."

"Mmmm…I like that. Let me taste that honey and see what it does."

I drag my tongue over her tender flesh covered in sweetness and suck her nipple into my mouth, loving how she moans above me. It only takes a few seconds of my mouth on her before she comes, just as she warned me she would.

Arching her back, she presses her body to mine at every point she can touch me, desperate to feel me against her as she comes. I watch in rapt attention as wave after wave of her orgasm ripples through her before kissing her hard.

"You look so fucking beautiful like this."

Her fingers scratch across the back of my shoulders as she pulls me to her. "I feel needy, like my body craves yours, Alex. I want you inside me."

I'd planned to play a lot more, but that can happen later. For now, she wants to be fucked, and I'm not a man to say no to that. "Whatever you want, baby."

I slip my arm around her to pull her to me as I sit

on the bed. A second later, I slide into that perfect cunt down to my balls while I press my lips to hers in a kiss meant to let her know how much I love being with her. We kiss wildly as the two of us desperate cling to one another and she rides my cock.

It's passion and need and desire all together, covered in sweetness like I've never experienced before. Kat pants against my lips with every time she takes every inch of me, and I take her breath inside my body, the two of us joined together in any way we can.

"Oh, God...Alex, I want to come so badly," she whimpers.

"Let yourself go, Kat. You're safe. I've got you," I say as her eyelids flutter closed.

She's close, and I revel in every tiny movement of her beautiful body that tells me at any second she's about to come. Rolling her hips, she begins to ride me faster, and then she stills after taking all of me inside her, and I feel her body milk my cock as her release washes over her.

For a long moment, I watch the gorgeous way every muscle softens in her face even as her body tenses and releases through her orgasm. My cock twitches once and then twice and then I come harder than ever before, filling her completely for the second time tonight.

Kat presses her mouth to mine in a satisfied kiss before sighing against my lips. "Oh, God. That was incredible."

I take a deep breath in and let it out in a rush before kissing her again. "It was, but I don't think you get to say I'm the sensual one anymore because you were there with me every inch of the way."

Her face lights up when I say that. "I was, wasn't I?"

While I watch her beam happiness as she realizes how incredible she is, I can't help but love seeing her like this. This is the Kat that lives deep inside her, protected by all that defensiveness she's built up around her.

This Kat makes me want something I've never wanted before.

KAT SIGHS, AND I REALIZE SHE'S LOOKING AT THE sunrise coming up outside my bedroom window. Pulling her to me, I press a kiss to her bare shoulder and smell her peach body lotion.

"Don't look out there. There's nothing for us outside this room. Outside this bed."

She rolls over and smiles at me. "Are you always this way? I don't think I've ever met anyone so sensual in my life."

"It's just who I am."

"It's not a bad thing at all," she says as she inches closer to my body. "I guess I'm just not used to it."

"Let's see if I can get you used to it," I say as I

snake my arm around her waist to pull her to me. My cock is rock hard and ready to go again for the third time since we got into this bed.

Not my most rounds of sex for a night, but sometimes quality is more important than quantity.

CHAPTER TWENTY

at

AFTER ALL THAT WHIPPED CREAM AND HONEY, NOT to mention the maraschino cherries Alex brought out for our third round of sex, we make our way to the shower to wash off all the stickiness. I've never used any of those things during sex with any other man, and now that I've experienced them, I'm not sure I can ever go back to sex without all that sweet stuff.

He turns on the shower and I step in, eager to rinse off. Maraschino cherries were fun in bed, although I suspect that white down comforter is going to need a professional cleaning, but all that red juice now makes me feel like I might stick to anything that gets close to me.

Alex steps in behind me and slides his arms around my waist, pulling me back against him. Unbelievably, he's hard again. This man's cock must be a machine!

I spin in his hold and look up at him in utter shock. "Does he ever rest? How can you be hard after all we did?"

With a devilish smile, he answers, "What can I say? He loves being inside you."

We've done everything but swing from the light fixture above his bed and me going down on him, so I stand on my tiptoes to kiss him on the lips and whisper against them, "Let's see how he likes this."

"If it's something to do with you, trust me, he's going to love it."

I slowly lower myself to the shower floor, crouching in front of him as he stands looking down at me with eyes full of anticipation. Running my hands over his thighs, I can't help but notice how gorgeous his legs are.

"You've got great legs," I say, tilting my head back to let the water wet my hair.

"You do too. I'm thinking it's a chef thing. All that hustling back and forth in the kitchen."

I think that's one of the best things about Alex. Now that I've seen the real him, I can honestly say he's completely ego-free. He takes compliments for what they are and gives them freely.

I've never met a man like him before. Either

they're insecure or they're egomaniacal. Not him, though. I love that.

His cock stands at attention, pressing against his abs and a tattoo of some kind of bird that takes up half the width of his stomach with its outstretched black wings. As I wrap my hand around the base, I ask, "What's the tattoo of?"

My question surprises him, and he laughs, shaking his head. "That's a strange question to ask right before you start sucking my cock. Which one? I've got a lot."

I roll my eyes and smile. "The one right where the head is hitting. You've told me about all the others but this one."

Alex looks down like he isn't sure what I mean and shrugs. "Oh, that's a raven."

While I begin to stroke up and down his shaft, I ask, "Any reason why you tattooed that right where your cock hits when you're hard?"

"Do you think a different bird would be better? Maybe a peacock?" he jokes.

That calls for another eyeroll. "No, silly. I was just curious."

As he begins to answer why he chose a raven for that very spot on his body, I take his cock into my mouth and gently suck the head. Whatever he was saying a second before suddenly fades away, and I look up to see his gaze utterly fixed on what I'm doing.

"Christ, you look so fucking beautiful like that. Take it all, baby."

I'm not sure I can since he's a pretty good length and width, but I do my best and leave my hand gripping the base as a little security just in case he thrusts his hips and sends his cock toward the back of my throat. He tastes sweet, likely a result of all that whipped cream, honey, and cherries from before. I like the flavor mixed with a hint of saltiness that's natural to him. It's sensual and earthy, very much like Alex.

I close my eyes as I focus on flicking my tongue along the underside of his shaft, but above me, he says in a low voice, "Open your eyes. Look at me."

It's a command I might chafe against with anyone else, but he sounds so sexy right now that I do as he orders. His eyes meet mine, and he slowly pushes his hips forward so his cock fills my mouth.

"That's it. I want to watch you watching me," he says low and deep, licking his lips to punctuate his words.

Hot water pours down over my head and face as I bob up and down on his cock, loving how sensual he looks watching me. I suck harder when I come back up to the top, and he moans in a way that sounds almost animalistic.

Alex March is pure sex through and through, and at this moment as I suck his cock, I can't get enough of this man.

He slides his hand over the top of my head and tightens his fingers in my hair as he says, "I want this to last a little longer than my body has planned, so I'm going to set the pace, okay?"

I'm not sure I have a choice in the matter, but I don't care, so I nod my agreement. He immediately slows me down and stops his thrusting until each time I take him into my mouth becomes a languid exploration of this part of his body.

Steam begins to surround us, and when I look up at him now, he looks like something from a dream. He's still as gorgeous as always, but his expression is far more intense than usual.

He lets me move my head back so he pops out of my mouth, and I ask, "Is anything wrong?"

With a smile, he shakes his head. "Not a thing. Why?"

"You looked different there."

"I was thinking I'd rather be inside that pretty cunt of yours than this. I've never been a blowjob kind of guy. It's too one-sided for my taste."

He says that like it's a bad thing. "I'm all for a change, if you want. I'd have to be crazy to say no to an offer like that."

"Good. Come up here so the two of us can enjoy ourselves."

When I stand up to my full height, he kisses me long and deep and then smiles against my lips. "Just in case you're wondering, I think you could change my mind about blowjobs."

"I don't mind them, if that's what you're worried

about. To be honest, that was probably the sexiest time I've ever had blowing someone. You get the credit for that."

Alex dips his head to kiss just below my ear and whispers, "Nothing about sex should be a job. Plus, I'd rather be doing something to give you pleasure."

He turns me around so the water isn't hitting my back anymore and the shower wall is behind me. When he eases me back against the tiles, they're cool and refreshing on my skin.

"Not to give you an ego trip, but I think you might be every woman's dream. We fantasize about men who want to please us because there aren't any in real life."

That makes him smile, and it's like the devil himself has let him borrow that grin of his. "Well, I'm right here in the flesh."

Cradling my face, he kisses my lips, sliding his tongue in to mingle with mine. It's erotic and makes me want to feel him between my legs again. I don't care how sore I am tomorrow. It will be well worth it.

I wrap my arms around his neck, and without a word spoken between us, he lifts me up to position me over his cock. As he slowly lowers me down onto it, I swear every nerve ending in my body is on high alert. He fills me completely, stretching my body to once again take every delicious inch of him.

This time, we don't say anything, but no words are needed as he slides in and out of me while the water rains down behind him. The tiles against my back loose their coolness with every time he thrusts into me and my body pushes up against the wall.

We're like two parts of one whole, two people so in tune with one another after only a few hours together that we easily fall into the rhythm of fucking. Alex's dark eyes stare into mine, and I sense he's searching for the answer to some unspoken question, but I don't ask like I normally would. I enjoy the silence, instead reveling in the feel of our bodies together giving the two of us pleasure.

When he pushes into me one last time and goes still, I feel him fill me with warmth. My orgasm follows soon after, my body milking his cock until there's nothing left inside him.

He holds me to him, and I hear his heavy breathing next to my ear. It's uniquely sexy and masculine. I gently stroke the back of his neck with my fingertips, loving how natural our time together feels. There is no worry about how I look or whether I did something he liked or didn't like during sex. He's completely real and transparent with how he feels and what he enjoys, almost as if it's second nature for him to tell a woman how much he loves being inside her or how beautiful she is as she's on her knees in front of him.

Finally, he whispers in my ear, "I think the water is starting to get cold."

I reach my hand out and feel it's turned lukewarm

already. "We outlasted the water heater," I say with a giggle.

"We better get all that sugar off us before we're standing in ice cold water," he says before kissing me sweetly on the lips.

When he eases out of me and sets me on my feet, I can't help feeling like I miss him, even though he's still just inches away from me. I look around for soap and see him hold up a white bar.

"Time to get clean, Kat."

He's cute and playful, and it makes me want to be more relaxed than I've ever allowed myself to be with a man. He lathers me up and then I lather him, while we spend time talking about what foods to use the next time we sleep together.

It's comfortable, more comfortable than I've ever been with another soul in my life. And I want more of it.

I want more of him.

AS MUCH AS I DON'T WANT TO LEAVE, WE BOTH HAVE to be on the set for nine this morning, and it's already after seven. So I turn out of his hold and roll out of bed, looking back to see him almost pouting.

Even that looks sexy on him.

"I wouldn't leave if we didn't have somewhere to be, but we do. I need to get home and get changed, or everyone's going to see me do the walk of shame right through the studio."

He sits up against the headboard and stretches his arms above his head. "I'll make you a deal. I'll wear what I wore last night, and we can both do the walk of shame onto the set."

While I look for my clothes strewn all over the floor, I shake my head and laugh. "That's no deal. You'll look like a guy who had a good time and people will high five you, and I'll look like some cheap slut and everyone will give me the side eye."

Alex cracks his neck and says, "It's not the fifties, Kat. Women are allowed to have sex."

I pick up my underwear and step into them. "True, but you'd be surprised at how attitudes aren't really that different. Everyone says they're great with women having sex, but the second you make it obvious that you do, things get weird. Trust me on this. You and I can walk into that studio smelling like sex, and only I will be the one dealing with judgment."

He reaches out to grab me when I lift my dress off the floor, and I fall onto the bed next to him. Staring down at me, he licks his lips and all I can think of is how talented he is with that mouth in so many ways.

"Seriously, come back to bed. We have enough time to have sex one or two more times. Then you can come back here tonight, and we'll pick up where we left off."

I love that he's making plans for us to get together

that night, but there's no way I can have sex with him even one more time and still make it home to get freshened up and get to the studio by nine. He does make it hard to say no to him, though.

"Alex, we can't. I want to, but we can't."

Taking my hand, he presses it against the sheet barely covering his erection. "Feel that. I'm ready to go now, and I bet I can get you ready in no time."

Before he can seduce me into staying by showing me his hard cock, I scramble to my feet and tug my dress over my head. This man is next to impossible to say no to.

"That doesn't look like you getting back into this bed," he says in a disappointed voice.

Finally dressed, I lean over and kiss him on that beautiful mouth of his. "I'm sorry. Can I take a rain check?"

Stuffing his hand into my hair, he pulls me down to kiss me hard, snaking his tongue into my mouth to tease me with what he wants to do again to my pussy. "Come back tonight. I'll make you dinner again, and then we can spend all night and all day tomorrow in bed since we don't have to be there all weekend."

How could a woman in her right mind say no to an offer like that coming from a man as beautiful and sexy as Alex? I'm not strong enough to say no, and the truth is, I don't want to. I'd stay in this bed having sex with him all day today if we could.

"Okay. I'll come over right after we get finished

with the show today. I just need to stop over at my place because I wasn't very prepared last night."

Alex's eyebrows climb into his forehead in a look of surprise. "So you weren't planning on sleeping with me? I think my ego is bruised hearing that."

"Do women usually sleep with you so quickly?" I ask, unsure if I want to know the answer.

A sheepish expression comes over him. "Well, not to brag, but yeah. Why shouldn't people have a good time if they enjoy one another's company?"

He's so confident about his sexuality that his answer doesn't offend me. Anyone else in the world could say that and I'd think he was a complete jackass.

But not Alex. I imagine there are many women like me too. He has a charm that can't be denied.

Just then, the memory of that beautiful woman from last night pops up in my brain. "I saw a gorgeous blonde with the longest legs I've ever seen in your hallway when I was waiting for you to answer the door. She looked at your apartment strangely. Is she an ex of yours?"

He thinks for a moment and then shakes his head. "I don't think so. I'm flattered that you think I've slept with all the women in my building, though."

"I didn't think that. I just wondered why she looked at your door oddly. That's all."

"Let's put it this way. If I liked her and she liked me, then we might sleep together. I like having a good time, and one of my favorite good times is sleeping with a beautiful woman. I'm a hedonist and proud of it. Life is for living, and I try to squeeze the most enjoyment out of it."

Jealousy spikes inside me, and I roll out of his hold to stand up next to the bed. "So Mr. Hedonist, does that mean you have a harem of women like me available at any time?"

Shaking his head, he smiles. "No. I've never been a one-woman man, but I don't make a habit of having a lot of women around if I'm seeing someone I really like. I really like you, Kat, so that means it's only you right now."

I need to get out of this bedroom before I say something stupid, so I give him a peck on the cheek and lean down to grab my shoes. "Good to know. Any idea what you're making us tonight?"

His gaze follows me as I walk around the bed to leave. "I don't know, but you'll love it, don't worry."

That streak of confidence a mile wide in him stops me as I open the door. Looking back at him, I take in one last eyeful of how gorgeous he looks there naked in bed after our lovemaking.

"Are you always this sure of yourself?"

"Only with two things. Food and fucking. Everything else in life is a crapshoot, to be honest."

"I'm going, but remember we're supposed to hate each other. So no giving me those eyes that made me want to sleep with you."

Alex throws his head back in laughter. "I promise I

won't give you those eyes if you promise you won't look at me like you did during dinner last night."

"Well, since I don't know what that means, maybe I won't look at you at all today. How's that sound?" I say, teasing him.

"I don't like it, but that'll keep us out of trouble, for sure."

"Today someone gets to enjoy the chicken bourguignon, so we'll be busy focused on that and watching some poor soul try that haggis. Oh, God, I hope it isn't me. I don't think I can even see that without throwing up."

"I think the ones who have to eat the food are the ones who decided what was going to be made, so I think I'll be fine. At least I hope I will," he says with a groan.

"I'll be thinking good thoughts for you. Maybe since Maria likes you she won't make you eat the haggis."

He gives me one of his sexy smiles, and I hurry out of his room, knowing if I don't leave now that I might never leave. This man has seduced and enchanted me.

I better watch out or I'm going to fall for him if he keeps acting like this.

AFTER THE SHORTEST SHOWER I'VE EVER TAKEN AND a quick swipe of mascara on my eyelashes, I hurry out of my apartment and race to the studio. I'm a few minutes late and Alex has already arrived, so at least we don't look like we were coming from the same place.

I get ready for the day at my station, and Shane comes to the center of the studio to announce who gets to eat which dish from yesterday. Murphy is the lucky one who will taste my dish, and Josie with the jet-black hair who's the quietest out of all of us has the misfortune of being chosen to eat the haggis.

Poor girl. What did she do to deserve that?

Emma seems particularly out of sorts today, not even saying hello when I came over and said good morning to her. Then it dawns on me why she's giving me the cold shoulder. I never got back to her last night.

Damnit!

I hurry over to her station and wait for her to finish setting up her area. When she does and still refuses to look at me, I say, "I'm sorry I didn't call you back last night. I got tied up and then it was too late. Please don't be angry."

She gives me a side-eyed look and frowns. "I just wanted to talk to someone after yesterday. It's no big deal."

"It is, and I'm sorry. If you'd like to talk after we're done today, we can grab a cup of coffee, if you want."

Her icy demeanor starts to defrost with my offer,

and she turns to look at me with a hint of a smile. "Okay. I'd like that. What tied you up last night?"

I know her question is innocent, but I can't help but grin when she asks it. Not a what. A who. A man who made me question what I'd been calling good sex all these years.

"Just a family issue. My parents have a ton of them," I lie.

She begins to say something about not being able to sleep after making that disgusting meal yesterday, but Maria barks out the order for everyone to go to their assigned dishes and start eating, so I hurry over to Alex's area to see what Murphy thinks of my creation. Alex has been assigned to eat an Indian dish that sounds downright tasty, so it's just me and Murphy there.

"Ready to have some chicken bourguignon?" I ask with a smile. "I hope you like it."

Murphy gives me a nod and then a big grin. "It smells great. You and Alex may hate each other, but you guys seem to be able to cook together, at least."

Stifling a laugh at how great we've turned out to be together, I shrug and hope my expression doesn't scream that I just came from an incredible night of sex with Alex. "Let's hope it tastes as good as it smells."

I watch him take his first forkful and wait for him to give me his opinion, but only a few moments later, his eyes open wide like he's terrified of something or someone and he falls to the floor clutching his stomach. I assume it's a joke since he's been pretty good with teasing all of us these past few days, but he doesn't get up.

"Murphy, what's wrong? Are you kidding or is this serious?" I ask as he contorts his body into a twisted shape that looks like utter agony.

I look up for help and see Shane standing a few yards away. "Shane! Something's wrong! Murphy collapsed. I think he needs an ambulance."

Maria rushes over with him and calls 9-1-1 while everyone else drops whatever they were doing and hurries to see what's going on. Murphy looks worse and worse as the seconds pass, and I can't help but worry this happened because of my dish.

"It's okay, Murph," Shane says, crouched down next to his head. "The ambulance is on its way, so you'll be fine."

But Murphy doesn't respond. I can't take my eyes off his pale skin near his mouth. What could have happened?

The paramedics arrive a few minutes later and shoo everyone away so they can work on him. Devastated, I walk over to my station and hope to God he's going to be okay. I can't imagine what could have caused him to collapse and writhe in pain like that.

Emma wraps her arm around my shoulders and whispers, "It's going to be okay. No matter what happened, he's going to be fine. Maybe he's allergic to something in the food you made, and he didn't tell anyone?"

Her suggestion makes me feel a little better, but then I see the paramedics place him on the stretcher and all I want to do is cry. I've never had anyone react that way to something I made. I'll never be able to cook again if he's not okay.

I see Alex give me a tiny smile from across the room and wish he could be here with me right now. He knows I didn't do anything wrong with that dish. Maybe if he could say something I wouldn't feel like everyone is looking at me like I'm some villain.

For the next hour, every contestant remains at their station, all of us silent after what we saw. I know it's probably just a guilty conscience, but with every passing minute, I feel like everyone, including Maria, is blaming me, like I intentionally did something terrible to the chicken bourguignon.

I hear Maria's phone go off, and it's Shane calling from the hospital. She puts it on speaker so we can all hear how Murphy is doing. "They're pumping his stomach right now. The ER doctor says he's sure he's been poisoned. He could smell it on Murph's mouth as soon as he walked in to examine him."

Every eye turns to look at me in judgment, and all I can do is shake my head. Poisoned? That's impossible. I made that dish exactly as the recipe said to. Nothing in that should have made him sick.

"Okay, thanks, Shane. I'll take care of things here.

Tell Murphy we're all worried about him and can't wait until he's better and back with us."

Maria immediately makes a beeline to where I stand horrified at the news we've all just heard. Gone is her usual kind expression she has with me, replaced by a look of pure anger. She thinks I did this to Murphy. Why?

"Kat, we can handle a lot of things on this show, as you well know. We love drama and conflict, but poisoning a contestant is beyond the pale. You're going to have to go."

I fight back tears as the room seems to close in on me. "What? You can't think this is my fault, Maria. I wouldn't do that. I wouldn't! Just like I wouldn't steal someone's knives, I would never poison anyone. There was nothing wrong with that dish when I finished making it yesterday. Alex can attest to that."

She looks over at him and he nods. "Maria, she made it perfectly. Trust me. Nothing in that was poisonous. Whatever got into that wasn't from Kat. I was standing right next to her the whole time."

But none of what he says convinces her.

"Security told me there was someone here last night after we all left to go home. I didn't learn about it until I showed up this morning. I didn't think anything of it, but now it all makes sense. You thought your dish was going to be eaten by Alex, didn't you, Kat?"

Tears well in my eyes as I try to answer her. "I…I

didn't know who would eat it. But I wouldn't poison anyone, including Alex. I swear!"

All around me people mumble, and it's all I can do to hold back my tears as I feel like I'm being indicted without any proof. I turn to look at Alex for help because all he has to do is tell Maria I couldn't have snuck in here last night since I was with him all night.

But he says nothing.

"You're off this show, Kat. You need to leave now," Maria says, her voice ice cold.

Shocked, I look over at Alex for help, but he simply winces. How could he do this to me? Did last night mean nothing to him?

I guess not since he can have anyone he wants. What's one woman and her problems when there's a world full of us and a million-dollar prize?

As tears begin to roll down my cheeks, security walks toward my station to escort me out of the building. I run out of the studio and down the hallway to the exit doors. I don't stop until I'm outside in the warm sunny day that's the complete opposite of what's happened to my life today.

Humiliated and unfairly accused, I've been expelled from the reality show. I won't have a chance to win that prize money or buy my own restaurant. All I get is to return to the job I hate and try to explain how I would never hurt anyone, much less poison someone, even for a million bucks.

Sobbing so hard my chest hurts, I don't hear Alex

come up behind me until he taps me on the shoulder. I spin around to see him looking at me with pure pity in his eyes.

Fuck, I hate pity.

"Why didn't you tell her there's no way I could have been here last night? You're my alibi, and you stood there and said not a single fucking word. Why?"

"We can't fraternize. It's in our contracts. You know that. If I said anything, then both of us would have been thrown off the show."

The way he says that like it's a completely logical answer to my desperately sad question makes me hate him all over again. "So it's a dog-eat-dog world out there, and you're going to make sure you get yours? Nice. Talk about making a girl regret sleeping with you."

"I'll talk to Maria and Shane and tell them there's no way you would have put anything into that dish. She said they're sending it off to a lab to find out exactly what Murphy ingested, so when they find out, they'll know it wouldn't have been you."

My emotions unspool inside me, and my tears begin to come harder now so I can barely see him. Pushing my hands against his chest, I snap, "I hate you, Alex March! I never want to see you and your selfish bullshit ever again!"

Before he can say another word, I throw open my car door, slamming it closed a second later. Nothing he could possibly say to me now is anything I want to listen to. Alex March is exactly the person I thought he was from the very beginning.

I was a fool to think any differently.

After wiping the tears from my eyes, I floor it out of the parking spot and drive away, glancing in the rear-view mirror only once to see him standing there looking as sad as I feel. He'll be fine. There's a planet full of women left for him to charm.

He'll get over me by day's end. If it takes that long.

As for me, I won't be over him so quickly because even though I keep telling myself I hate him, the truth is I don't. And that's the part that hurts the most.

Alex and Kat's story continues in Desirous!

ABOUT THE AUTHOR

K.M. Scott writes contemporary romance stories of sexy, intense, and unforgettable love. A New York Times and USA Today bestselling author, she's been in love with romance since reading her first romance novel in junior high (she was a very curious girl!). Under her Gabrielle Bisset name, she write paranormal and historical romance. She lives in Pennsylvania with a herd of animals and when she's not writing can be found reading or feeding her TV addiction.

Be sure to visit K.M.'s Facebook page at **https://www.facebook.com/kmscottauthor** for all the latest on her books, along with giveaways and other goodies! And to hear all the news on K.M. Scott books first, sign up for her newsletter today and be sure to visit her website at **http://www.kmscottbooks.com**

BOOKS BY K.M. SCOTT

HEART OF STONE SERIES

Crash Into Me (Heart of Stone #1)

Fall Into Me (Heart of Stone #2)

Give In To Me (Heart of Stone #3)

Heart of Stone Volume One

Ever After (Heart of Stone #4)

A Heart of Stone Christmas (Heart of Stone #5)

Return To Me (Heart of Stone #6)

Forever With Me (Heart of Stone #7)

Heart of Stone Volume Two

Hard As Stone (Heart of Stone #8)

Set In Stone (Heart of Stone #9)

Silent As A Stone (Heart of Stone #10)

Heart of Stone Volume Three

All of Me (Heart of Stone #11)

CLUB X SERIES

Temptation (Club X #1)

Surrender (Club X #2)

Possession (Club X #3)

Satisfaction (Club X #4)

PROJECT ARTEMIS SERIES

In The Darkness (Project Artemis #1)

After The Storm (Project Artemis #2)

Behind The Scenes (Project Artemis #3)

Project Artemis Box Set

FINDING THE ONE SERIES

Hard Work (Finding The One #1)

Big Love (Finding The One #2)

DIRTY BOSS SERIES

Sweet Things (Dirty Boss #1)

Private Secretary (Dirty Boss #2)

Play Date (Dirty Boss #3)

Dirty Boss Volume One

K.M.'S BOOKS ARE IN AUDIOBOOK TOO!

BOOKS BY K.M. SCOTT WRITING AS GABRIELLE BISSET

SONS OF NAVARUS SERIES

Vampire Dreams Revamped (A Sons of Navarus Prequel)

Blood Avenged (Sons of Navarus #1)

Blood Betrayed (Sons of Navarus #2)

Longing (A Sons of Navarus Short Story)

Blood Spirit (Sons of Navarus #3)

The Deepest Cut (A Sons of Navarus Short Story)

Blood Prophecy (Sons of Navarus #4)

Blood Craving (Sons of Navarus #5)

Blood Eclipse (Sons of Navarus #6)

Blood Ascendant (Sons of Navarus #7)

The Sons of Navarus Box Set #1

The Sons of Navarus Box Set #2

DESTINED ONES DUET

Stolen Destiny (Destined Ones Duet #1)

Destiny Redeemed (Destined Ones Duet #2)

VICTORIAN EROTIC ROMANCES

Love's Master

Masquerade

The Victorian Erotic Romance Trilogy